Dial K for Kiss

for

TANYA EAVENSON

Cover design by Chautona Havig

Edited by Elizabeth Kitchens

Dial K for Kiss / Tanya Eavenson —1st ed.

On file at the Library of Congress in Washington, DC.

Ebook ISBN: 978-1-945981-14-2

Print ISBN: 978-1-945981-18-0

Dedication

This book wouldn't have been possible without the Lord, whose love never ceases, and His mercies are new every morning.

To my dear friends April Gardner and Elizabeth Kitchens, for their encouragement and support.

I'd also like to give a shout-out to Joy Melville, Erralee Hendrian, and Angie Eads, for helping me name my characters. As you're reading *Dial K for Kiss*, you might even see their names mentioned within the story. Thank you, ladies!

And to my readers, this book is for you. I hope you enjoy Julia and Andrew's story as much as I loved writing it.

"It is of the LORD's mercies that we are not consumed, because his compassions fail not. They are new every morning: great is thy faithfulness."
Lamentations 3:22–23

Series

Prologue

Five-year-old Julia Morgan nibbled on the edge of her lip as she crouched behind the monkey bars. She wasn't really hidden, but she didn't know where else to go.

"Run, Julia! Andrew sees—" Courtney squealed as one of the other boys appeared from behind a shrub and grabbed her arm.

"Got you," he shouted, triumphant.

Julia took off running, scanning the playground for a good spot to go unnoticed but coming up empty.

Another squeal and shout drew Julia's gaze over her shoulder. Beth had been caught as well, and the boys were pulling her friends out of sight, probably to their "boys only" headquarters.

It was up to her now. The girls could win if she didn't get caught. She continued to the far side of the playground, where a group of kids hung out around the fence. She darted behind them and, trying to blend in, knelt in the dirt. A rock pressed against her knee, but she ignored it and craned her neck to see where Andrew had gone. He was rounding the double slide, stalking the playground like a hunter in the woods.

Since she was only five, her dad never let her do anything when they went hunting, only sit in their hunting blind and watch the deer, but the last time, her mom had gone out of town, and he'd taken her tracking with him. Now, she felt like she was that hunted deer.

"Julia! Game's over!" Andrew's hazel eyes swung from right to left, searching. "We have to go in now. It's snack time."

Already? Had they been playing that long? The group of kids she knelt behind ran toward the classroom door, leaving her out in the open.

Andrew's gaze caught hers, and a satisfied smirk filled his face. "There you are."

As he neared, she dodged toward the fence gate. He countered. She tried to move away again, but he shifted with her. She huffed deeply, trying to catch her breath, and put her hands on her hips in frustration. "I thought you said it was time to go in."

"I did, but you won't get away. I'll chase you for as long as it takes." He jumped onto the fence gate and swung toward her to block her from getting away.

She tried to run but the gate collided with her face, and the impact threw her onto the ground. Pain slammed both sides of her head, and tears filled her eyes.

Andrew stood over her now, a frown marring his face. "Julia, your forehead's bleeding bad."

"My head hurts." She reached to touch the spot, but Andrew caught her hand.

"You'll get it dirty."

At his words, her stomach became queasy. "I don't feel good."

His lips flattened, and his brows dipped before he looked away. "Teachers are coming." He dropped her hand.

"Julia!" Mrs. Dunlap rushed to her side. "Oh dear. Let's get you inside so we can take a look at your boo-boo."

Julia whimpered as her teacher lifted her into her arms. Mrs. Dunlap carried her through the yard and into the room where they took naps and set her down gently on her cot. She hurried to a box of tissues on her desk, nabbed a few, and came back. "Let's put these on your forehead for a moment while I get a washcloth to clean the area. Hold the tissues for me." She looked away, gaze searching. "I'll find Mrs. Bright to call your parents." She hurried away.

How bad was it for her parents to be called? Andrew hadn't even let her touch it. She could barely hold the tissues against her skin.

Andrew crept through the door, his focus following where Mrs. Dunlap had gone, then settled on the edge of her cot. His eyes narrowed on her forehead. "Are you okay? It looks bad. You have blood on your new shirt."

"How do you know it's a new shirt?"

"I've never seen it before."

She looked down at the blue flowered print her mom had brought back from her trip to France last week but seeing the blood drips on the fabric caused nausea to bubble in her throat.

"It hurts?"

Afraid to speak for fear she'd become sick all over Andrew's shoes, she squeaked out, "Yes."

"Can I kiss your head and make it feel better?"

"No!" She jolted with shock, then winced at the pain. "You'll hurt me worse."

"Then on your mouth. That's how Daddy makes Mommy's hurts go away." He leaned forward and pressed his lips hard against hers before pulling away. "Better?"

She blinked, assessing. "I don't think so. It still hurts. Is it still bleeding?"

He stood and cocked his head at her. "Yep. Bad too. I think the tissues are stuck to it."

"Andrew!" Mrs. Dunlap startled them both. "Out with you now." She was at the cot in three steps and turned Andrew with a small push toward the door.

He complied, looking back at Julia as he went.

One

Though the alarm blared, Julia awoke with a lazy smile on her lips and a light chuckle in her throat. The many "first kiss" stories her local radio station, Kiss 100, was gathering from their listeners was the culprit. Even at age thirty-seven, it wasn't a surprise she'd dreamt of Andrew.

As she tapped "dismiss" on her phone's alarm, she had to admit she was enjoying the stories, even if her dreams were replaying moments from thirty-two years ago as she slept. And telling her sister of her nightly escapades had been a mistake. No amount of convincing on her sister's part was going to get Julia to call her story in, especially to the man who'd kissed her in the first place.

Andrew Larsen, now known on the radio as Drew, was becoming a household name, and she didn't want any part of his upcoming status or popularity. They were as different as night and day, and they always had been. He'd been popular, enjoying the spotlight, where she hung back with the lesser-known crowd and was determined to change the world, one life at a time. Things hadn't changed much it seemed, but with the selling of her family's tech company and investing in a local nonprofit, she was on her way to living her heart's desire.

Julia's phone lit up on the nightstand. She leaned over to see if it was the director of the community garden—they had a meeting within the hour—but it was her sister, Kaylie.

Call me!

Julia pressed the palm of her hand against her eye and ran it across her cheek. What type of emergency could her sister have that she'd text instead of call? One that could wait.

She texted back. *I'm hopping in the shower. Give me 15 minutes.*

Setting her phone down on the dresser, she'd only taken a few steps toward the bathroom when her phone chimed harps and lute. The elf-sounding ringtone her sister picked out because of her love for *The Lord of the Rings* movies drew Julia back to the phone. She snatched it up and answered, and her sister immediately started talking over her.

"Tap your Kiss app and listen. Drew is beating you to the punch."

Julia's thoughts scrambled and clung to a thread of disbelief and fear. "He wouldn't." She tapped the phone's screen, and Drew's voice rose clear. Her mind raced back to her dream. But this wasn't a dream.

"The gate had too much momentum. It collided against her forehead and sent her to the ground. My little boy's heart broke at seeing blood on her face. I remember standing in front of her, and when she didn't say a word, tears started filling her soft brown eyes. It was the first time I ever recall feeling lost and hopeless, knowing what I'd done."

"Awww, Julia, how sweet," Kaylie cut in. "I prefer his version of the story. Soft brown eyes."

"That's because you're a romantic, and I was the one gushing blood everywhere."

"Caller, you're on the air," Drew said.

"Hey Drew, this is Bethany. How old were you when you first kissed that girl?"

"I was six, and she was five. I guess you can say I robbed the cradle." He chuckled. "Next caller. You're on the air."

"Drew, this is Tammy. My question is, what was her name? Do you remember?"

"This might surprise you, but I do. Sorry. That's all I'm going to say."

"Are you sure you can't tell us?"

"Tammy, you know it wouldn't be right to kiss and tell. Besides, I'm a gentleman. Thanks for your call."

Julia sighed. "Actually, that's what he's doing. Doesn't he know what 'kiss and tell' means?"

Her sister laughed.

"Now, where were we?" Drew continued. "We're standing there, her bleeding and me guilty for causing her pain, when a teacher comes over and swoops her up and carries her away. It wasn't long before I found my friend on a cot where we took naps. I waited in the corner behind a fake plant for the teacher to leave, and when she did, I snuck to my friend's side and sat on the edge of her cot. I told her how sorry I was for what happened. I honestly thought it would make the tears go away, but no matter what I said, my words didn't help. I still felt like I had to do something, so I asked if I could kiss her." He chuckled. "I can't remember her response, but I kissed her lips so fast, my head started spinning when I stood up. She was my first and last crush."

"What?" Kaylie asked, her voice raising a notch. "What's he mean by that? His first and *last*?"

"I don't know," Julia said, though her thoughts jumped to the same question. But whatever he was thinking, whatever he meant, she'd quit trying to decipher those words long ago. "I've got to get ready for my meeting. I've wasted enough time as it is." Yet, when the next caller asked what Drew meant about crushes, and if he'd seen her over the years, a need drew her to hear his response.

"After that day she was withdrawn from the preschool. I learned she moved away, but she moved back my junior year of high school. I knew it was her because she had a heart shaped freckle on her jawline right under her ear. As a kid, I was fascinated by it. Anyway, she was in my TV Productions class. We ran in different circles, and after graduation night, we never saw each other again. I can honestly say that I've never forgotten her. How could you forget your first kiss?"

Julia closed the app, her pulse tapping away. She gave that freckle a glancing touch, then cleared her throat. "Kaylie, I gotta go."

"Shhh. The listeners are pushing him for more information."

"Bye." Julia hung up, dumped the phone on her bed, and hurried into the bathroom.

After she'd readied herself for the day, she grabbed her planner and keys from her desk and forced her thoughts onto her meeting with the Fletcher County council members. She and the nonprofit board members would be discussing the community garden. Whatever the day held, it could *not* be thoughts of the man who'd stood on her doorstep on graduation night.

Two

"Drew, my man! That was awesome. Let's talk. Walk with me." The station manager, Michael, held the sound booth door open as he was leaving. Drew followed him to a small cubicle he used when he needed an office. His boss leaned against the edge of the desk. "I know your "Kiss and Tell Time" is set to wrap up at the end of the week, but what do you say about extending it? This idea of yours, for listeners to call in their first kiss stories, was ingenious. It's been two weeks and people are still calling."

Why did he keep calling it "Kiss and Tell Time"? It made it sound so cheap. The stories shared across the airways were true stories, shared in fun, and to some, it meant a great deal. Even today, Drew shared his first kiss story, and it was quite personal. He'd almost backed out, but it was worth the risk.

But Michael understood Drew's desire to leave the mid-morning time slot and move to the *Morning Rush*. This was Drew's chance, and the idea he'd pitched to Michael was paying off. Nothing was going to get in his way, especially himself. Whatever Michael wanted to call it was fine by him. Who was he to argue with the boss?

"Thank you, Michael." Drew tapered his smile as he set his backpack in the chair tucked in the corner of the office. "I certainly appreciate the opportunity to prove myself for the position."

Michael nodded. His mouth twitched into a sly smile as his gaze held Drew's like a skillful prosecutor's. "Yes, well, that was my thought exactly. The man for the job will need to prove himself in more ways than one. Are you that man, Drew? Up for the challenge?"

Drew instinctively stood taller, his mind racing. "Absolutely. I'm your guy."

"I was hoping my sixth sense was right where you were concerned. So, tell me, since you started this "Kiss and Tell Time," which day do you think we received the most callers?"

"Today. The moment I started talking about Julia, the phones lit up." He grinned to himself at the thought of her. He'd never forgotten the shock in her warm chocolate-colored eyes after he'd kissed her.

"Julia, was it? What a story. It certainly took me by surprise, as I think it did our listeners. The unexpected sells."

Well, the only thing Drew was trying to sell was himself, and his ideas.

Last week, one of the *Morning Rush* hosts got married and quit, leaving a coveted host spot available for the taking. Drew planned to be the taker.

"This Julia person . . . do you know her well?"

At the question, Drew crossed his arms against his chest. "We've not seen each other since high school or spoken since then."

"But you do know her?"

He nodded, not liking where this was going. "Yes. But that was years ago." Michael's eyes brightened with excitement, but Drew's jaw tightened, and he forced his mouth closed.

Michael rose from the corner of the desk and grinned. "I see I've touched on something personal. Even better. There's nothing like having skin in the game."

"What are you asking me to do, Michael?"

"I want you to find Julia and convince her to date you. Not only will our listeners love the snapshot of the two of you together, but I can also contact our affiliate television stations to video your dates."

"Record? Our dates? Plural?"

"Of course. For a month's time. We're going to milk this childhood, high school romance for all it's worth."

"I never said anything about romance."

"Didn't need to. The working of your jaw, the frantic look in your eyes. Your visceral movements a moment ago spoke volumes. Am I wrong? Tell me I'm wrong."

Drew gave an abrupt, sardonic laugh. "I didn't know I needed a defense attorney."

A satisfied smile settled on Michael's face. "I know, I should have been an attorney. Anyway, we're interviewing someone for the morning show position tomorrow. You have some competition, Drew, but with my vote, you'll be a shoe in. Can I count on you to make this happen?"

Drew took a steady breath, and before he could change his mind, he gave a nod. "I'll find her."

"I knew I liked you. You've been on my radar for some time. It's good to know I wasn't wrong about you." He clapped Drew on his shoulder. "But this isn't about finding her, you need to convince her to date you for a month. Not for a week or two, an entire month."

"She has a life, Michael. A very successful one at that. She might not have time for me. Maybe she's seeing someone. Engaged." At the words, his throat formed a knot.

"I don't care if you go as friends, but I want this, Drew. And somehow, I think you'll be able to convince her to help you. We'll extend your "Kiss and Tell Time" for another two weeks. That should give you enough time to find and convince Julia." He squeezed Drew's shoulder before leaving the cubicle. On the way out, he paused and faced him again. "Each week, I want to see you together, at least twice—one will be a date night with cameras rolling. I don't care what you do. Talk it out with her, but you keep me informed."

Drew's gaze trailed after Michael until he disappeared down the corridor. He couldn't describe the numbing sensation trickling through his body. How would he convince Julia to date him when there was so much between them? Too much, she would say, not that he could even name what they'd been to each other.

And that was the problem. They were too different. During high school, she was the soft spoken one, beautiful, intelligent, where he was loud, popular, and smart enough to know, even back then, they didn't belong together. He wasn't good enough for her. And yet, he'd never forgotten what it was like being with her.

Maybe it was a little crazy, but he'd followed her career, and when she'd made the cover of *Forbes*, he'd been happy for her. He'd thanked the Lord for her family's success, which had turned into hers alone after their passing. She'd grown her family business into a multi-million dollar tech company.

And now he was supposed to reach out after all this time and ask to date her?

Julia was in a league of her own, and who was he? A radio talk show host who was still chasing his dreams. At least that was one dream he still believed he could reach.

Three

Julia jabbed her spade into the untilled soil with precision. She'd heard that gardening was good for the soul; she just didn't realize *how much* until the neighboring city had turned down her proposal to extend her garden into their county. It had been two weeks since that, and she still felt the rejection. She was ready to invest her own capital in the project, but they weren't willing to give up the land. But with the new fiscal year, she could change their minds, but how?

She looked to the next block, at the rundown drug house the city was finally able to purchase. The pale green paint coloring the exterior seemed to crack in every direction, and most sections of paint fell to the tall weeds beneath. Slated to take its place was a row of upscale family apartments.

She'd had some concerns that the two-block area housing the community garden would be moved or torn down permanently, but when she heard from the city about their plans for the apartments, she was thankful she'd incorporated a neighborhood park along with a walking trail around the perimeter of the garden. She had plans to do the same in the neighboring county and extend her garden there. If only she could get enough support for the project. Maybe she could find a way to get more eyes on what they were doing for the community.

Jabbing the soil again, she viewed the last unused area still available for planting. The Cooperative Extension Services soil testing stated that this smaller patch wasn't as fertile as the rest, and it might be more difficult to produce anything from it. But the homeless population and food insecurity was growing, so she was willing to try.

"Julia."

She startled as someone called her name. "Sorry," she said, turning to the man a few paces away. "I was lost in—" Rocking back on the heels of her sneakers, she shaded her eyes from the sun with a gloved hand. She squinted, unsure if she was seeing correctly. *It can't be.* "Andrew?" she murmured.

"Hey, Julia. I was hoping to find you here."

His words were said in such a casual tone, as if they'd been in each other's company only yesterday, but it had been twenty years. Half those years had left her wondering where he was, how he was doing, and if he'd ever married. The other half had answered her questions as she'd heard his voice on the radio. A voice she listened to when she could from ten in the morning to two in the afternoon.

She blinked a few times, her mouth going dry as she gathered herself for a coherent thought or two. Or at least a response to his greeting. "Andrew," she said again, with more volume and with surprise clear in her tone.

Not exactly what she planned to say to him if they ever saw each other again. It was odd hearing his name on her lips, but it felt familiar. Heat rose to her cheeks as she realized she was staring. She hurried to her feet and threw down her spade like a ninja star, sticking it to the dirt.

He peered down at the spade. "Maybe I should talk to you about being my bodyguard." He grinned, meeting her gaze. For a tick of time, she was back in high school, taken in by the lift of his lips, the right corner rising slightly before the left followed. The lazy smile, the easy way he held himself, was just as she remembered, but he was no longer a boy. By the pull of his shirt and strength in his arms, the man standing before her had filled out in width and muscle. His jaw was more defined, his hazel eyes more inquisitive as he watched her, and his deeper voice rumbled through her now in a way it hadn't when they'd been young.

She didn't know what to do with her hands and wished she hadn't thrown her gardening tool to the ground. "You wanted to speak with me?" She wiped the sweat from her brow with her shirt sleeve.

"I did. You're a hard woman to track down."

She looked around, seeing if anyone was watching them, but no one paid them any mind. It wasn't strange for her to have visitors in the garden area. Sometimes she held meetings here to showcase what they were doing, so certainly to everyone else, it was business as usual. The fact gave her brain a small sense of calm, though her heart was tripping over itself with every beat. "We can talk at the bench over there." She removed her gloves and pointed to an area away from the volunteers working in the collard greens.

"Sounds good. It will give us some privacy."

It must have been important for Andrew to be here, and whatever he had to say, she didn't want anyone to overhear. "How did you know where to find me?"

They reached the bench, and Andrew waited for her to be seated before he sat alongside her. "Finding a multi-million-aire in an urban community in Alabama isn't as difficult as you might think. It was the timing that was hard. So how have you been?"

She laughed at the bizarre question. "You searched me out after all these years to ask how I've been? I've been good. How have you been?"

He grinned. "Well, I see what you mean. I've been good."

Julia set her gloves at her side and folded her hands in her lap. She wasn't comfortable with small talk. She wasn't comfortable with him being here. Why was he here? "Since we've both been good, why don't you tell me why you wanted to find me."

Andrew cocked his head slightly and studied her for a brief moment. "You've changed."

Julia shied away, hiding her face from him, and looked off in the distance to the passing cars. She wanted to agree with his assessment, but it wasn't true. Not really. Oh, she might have changed outwardly, as Andrew had, and was more assertive from time to time when the need arose, but she was still the girl with the sweaty palms and weak knees when she was around the guy next to her. "Not really."

"I disagree. I see a confidence in you that never existed before."

She fought the urge to shrug her shoulders and met his gaze instead. "I think that confidence you're seeing was built out of necessity after my parents passed and the family business fell into my lap. At twenty-four, I had a choice to make: allow my family's hard work to fail or help it to grow and reach its potential."

"And you grew alongside the company."

"I did." She went silent, thinking back over the years, the struggles, the tears. "It was through the hardships that I found my passion."

Andrew's brow furrowed slightly as if her words affected him, but before she could ask, he looked to the garden. "In helping others."

"How did you know?"

His features softened as his eyes sought hers. "I saw glimpses in you during high school, even in preschool. You were always kind, Julia. So, tell me, what made you decide to sell the company?"

She was still curious as to what she'd said for his expression to have changed, but not wanting to bring up the past more than they were, it was better to answer his questions, so he'd share why he was here. "It was hard running the company and doing my community work. It stretched me in ways that at times were good, and others, not so good. Then I met a homeless woman, and everything changed for me."

"How so?"

Julia looked to her hands. "You didn't come to hear me rattle on. There was a point to your visit."

"How about we compromise? You finish telling me about how things changed for you, and then it will be my turn to tell you why I'm here. Agreed?"

"What if I insist?"

"Saying that sentence shows me you've changed."

Uncomfortable with the way he was looking at her, as if he was trying to uncover some kind of mystery, she hurried to answer, "The woman is a veteran. She struggled to survive after returning to the States and couldn't transition well into society. She started doing drugs to cope. After a time, she lost everything, her marriage, her family, and her freedom—she eventually landed in jail. The day she was released was the day we met. She was clean by then, but she had nowhere to go and no one to take her in. She had no money, nothing to eat. I knew I had to do something."

"What happened to her?"

"I found her a place to stay, then I took it a step further. I reached out to the nonprofit I'm connected to. We joined forces and opened a department within the organization to help people who are homeless or in need of a helping hand, especially vets, get back on their feet. The money I donate goes to financially support those who help with the gardening projects. Then there are volunteers who give their time."

Andrew scanned the garden, where a group of volunteers were watering and pruning. "Is your vet here today?"

"She is," Julia said, unable to hide her smile. "Now she

volunteers her time. She's on her feet again. You asked me why I sold. The experience opened my eyes to what the Lord wanted, what I could do with the financial gifts He'd given me. And if I sold the company, I could do more for His glory. Now, if only I could convince the city in the next county for a piece of land to duplicate the garden, I could do even more. If I had enough interest, they might at least take my proposal seriously."

"What's this? What proposal?"

"I proposed that if the city would give me two blocks of land in their low-income area, I'd provide the capital through fundraising as well out of my own pocket to develop it, plus I'd provide the plans for a park and garden for the community. It would be a mirror image of what we have here, but it was turned down."

"Did they say why?"

"There wasn't enough interest, but they'll be accepting new proposals for the upcoming year soon." She looked to her hands, feeling anxious all of a sudden. "Andrew, why did you drive from Birmingham to sit on my bench?"

Four

Andrew.

He couldn't remember the last time someone had called him by his real name, and each time Julia spoke it, a need lingered within his chest. He knew what that need was; he had battled it for years. But now that he was with her again, about to bare his soul, he was fearful of how this was going to play out.

"Well, I need to get back to the garden." She stood, her back rigid. Her dark ponytail swayed where it hung midway down her frame. "It was good seeing you again. After all this time."

Her voice lowered at the last of her words, and he knew he deserved the jab, the reminder of what he'd done. He'd left her waiting for him with promises he never kept, and now here he was, showing up out of the blue, unable to tell her why he'd come. No, he couldn't blame her, but as she took a step to leave, then another, he knew he had to stop her.

He stood. "I need your help." The plea came out breathless as he watched her stop, her back remaining to him. "It's a long story. I'm not even sure where to begin."

"Highlights, then." She turned those brown eyes on him, the same ones he'd found himself lost in over the years. He'd always been aware of her, as he was now, and time did nothing to stop his feelings where she was concerned. Michael had no idea what he was asking him to do.

"I'm up for a promotion at the radio station Kiss 100, and

in trying to impress the station's higherups, I suggested we host listeners' first kiss stories."

"Yes, my sister and I have enjoyed them."

"You've been listening?" A sense of satisfaction filled his chest, but did she know he'd shared their story? If the blush tinting her cheeks was any indication, she had heard, though she didn't answer him. "I shared our story the other day, and the listeners loved it. So did the station manager. He offered me the morning position under one condition—that I convince you to date me for a month."

She didn't move. "Date *you* for a month?"

"I know I have no right to ask. But there's more."

"How much more?"

"He wants two dates per week, and one of those dates must be . . . recorded or televised."

She crossed her arms against her chest. "I can't, Andrew. You know I dislike the spotlight, and I'm using *dislike* lightly."

"I know." He wanted to go to her but forced his feet to remain in place. "If this wasn't important, I wouldn't be here." He shook his head to himself, knowing this was a bad idea. He ran his fingers through his hair. He'd never thought it would come to this, that his own merit and hard work wouldn't count in the long run.

"I'm sorry, Andrew. I really am, but it's not going to happen."

His feet moved to place him directly in front of her. "Can you at least think about it? Pray about it? I've given up so much in my life for this opportunity." *If only she knew.*

"Do you know what you're asking me?"

Yes, the same Michael requested of me. He began to pace. "If there was some way to make it up to you, I would. I'd even help you raise interest in your garden project." He stopped, his words echoing in his mind. He inhaled a sharp breath. "I know how to move the spotlight from you, if you agree. We'll use the televised dates to focus on the garden."

She shook her head, took a few steps from him, and stopped. Long moments ticked by before she finally spoke. "Will your station manager go for it?"

"We don't need to tell him exactly. He said he didn't care what we do, but to talk it over with you. I think as long as we're together, he'll be satisfied."

"I don't know about this, Andrew. There's no guarantee it will work." She began wringing her hands, a sure sign his plea was working. One more push and she'd agree.

"You're right, there are no guarantees, but I believe together we can pull this off. You'll get more eyes on your garden project, and I'll have my dream job. We can do this, Julia." Without thinking, he cupped her hands. His heart jolted at the feel of her after all these years, and his breath hitched. Her hands stilled within his, and her attention trained on him. An expression flitted across her features that he couldn't read, but the idea he had the power to soothe her touched him deeply.

She slowly removed her palms from his. "Care to see the garden?"

His thoughts dissipated. Did she mean . . .? "If you'd like to show it to me."

"I think it would be for the best. You'll need to familiarize yourself with where things are since you'll be joining me every Monday." She gave him a hesitant smile, an answer before the question was even voiced.

"I need to hear the words, Julia. Does this mean you'll do it?"

"Yes, as long as you keep your word in helping the garden attract more attention." The sorrowfulness behind her beautiful eyes seemed to grow.

Could this be a way for him to make up for the past? If he

proved to her that he was a man of his word, maybe the hurt and disappointment he'd caused them both all those years ago would finally fade. "I'll help any way I can." He was about to say more, but motion in his peripheral drew his focus.

"Ms. Morgan." A man's voice broke through the air and stole the moment between them. He gestured her toward a group of volunteers. "If we can steal you for a moment."

"I'll be right there." She waved and turned back to Andrew with a decisive nod, as if needing to reassure herself. "I'm going to enjoy the month. And my new free helper."

"I see how it is." He gave her a playful smile, hoping to lighten the mood. "Let's go meet this crew of yours."

What was she thinking? How could she have agreed to spend time with Andrew for the next month, and on TV?

Julia fumbled with her keys as she opened her apartment door. *Lord, his pleading. His touch. Was this your plan, or did I jump in feet first?*

She closed and locked the door behind her, set her purse on the foyer table, and headed for the kitchen. Placing both her hands on the countertop, she leaned over in a breath of released air and inhaled deeply. "You're not going to hyper-ventilate," she told herself as she began a pattern of inhaling, then exhaling.

Of course, she sounded sure of herself most of the time, always in business meetings and in dealings with city officials, or with the community at large, but why couldn't she show that same side of herself in front of Andrew? She could barely sit with him on the bench. These were going to be the longest weeks of her life. The worst part of it, he still mattered to her after all these years. She felt it not only in her heart but at his touch when he covered her hand with his.

"Breathe, Julia. You can do this. With your sister's help." She grabbed her cell from her purse and dialed.

Julia didn't wait for her sister's greeting. "Hey, I need to talk."

"Hey, to you too. What's going on?"

"Are you free for lunch?"

"With the kids in school again, all I need to do is ship off a few orders, and then I can meet you someplace."

"How about eleven, at the coffee shop that looks over the park? I missed breakfast, and they serve omelets until one."

"Great. See you then."

Julia ended the call and hurried to shower and dress, all the while trying to come up with a way to tell her sister about her agreement with Andrew.

She thought she'd figured it out, but as she set aside the menu later that morning and looked up at her sister, her mind went blank.

"Julia, what is it? First of all, you call me for lunch, when we both know I'm the one who calls you. Second, that frightened look, the raised-brow thing you're doing is bad enough, but your silence . . . Thirdly, I know that look. What have you done?"

Julia's thoughts were so jumbled, she wasn't sure how she was going to get them out, but then, as if someone turned on the water spigot, the words rushed out. "Andrew Larsen approached me with a proposition to date him for a month with cameras rolling to help him clinch the position as the new morning show host at Kiss 100." Her sister's eyes widened, but Julia continued as the words drained from her mouth. "In return, he'll help me get more eyes on my garden, and hopefully between us both, influence the city's decision to approve my proposal before the fiscal vote."

She waited for her sister to say something, but when she didn't, Julia took a drink of water and cleared her throat, ready to say something, anything. "Kaylie."

"I want to laugh because this sounds like a joke, but you're being totally serious."

"I am."

The waitress came with their omelets and coffees. "Do you ladies need anything else?"

"I think this is it." Kaylie lifted her water glass. "But if you happen to have any *good judgment* lying around in the back, I think my sister can use some." She took a sip.

"Kaylie," Julia said under her breath.

The waitress fought a smile but failed miserably She glanced between them before addressing her sister. "If I find any, I'll be sure to bring it out."

Kaylie set her glass down. "Thank you. There will be an extra tip in it for you too." Kaylie shook her head before digging into the breakfast. "I don't know what you were thinking," she said around a mouthful of eggs.

"I was thinking about the garden."

"And dating Drew."

"That's not fair. You know how hard I've worked to establish this garden imprint within the community. It has always been my goal, my heart's desire to make a difference."

"Drew was your goal and heart's desire once."

"That was a long time ago, Kaylie. My feelings have changed." She looked away from her sister and knew it was a mistake the moment she did. She'd given herself away. She tried to recover by picking up her water glass, but her sister's gaze said she wasn't fooled.

"I was in Italy at the time, so I don't know what happened that night after graduation, but you've always been tight-lipped about it. Whatever it was that went on between you and Drew, it was never resolved. You can't blame me for being concerned. You're my sister, and I don't want you to be pressured into something you're not ready for."

"I'm okay with this."

"Are you sure about that? You're going to be in the spotlight. On TV, for the world to see. You don't like the limelight, and you're scared to death of cameras."

"I can take pictures all day long."

"Not that type of camera, and you know it. I can still recall the moment you were walking down the runway in your first Giorgio Armani gown and froze at the sight of the cameramen videoing."

"I was fifteen, a nervous little girl with so much pressure on her shoulders. What can I say? My older sister was a hard act to follow."

"But you never got over the fear. It was your *first* anxiety attack."

Julia took a large bite of her omelet to give her a moment to think about how to respond. It was useless. "What am I going to do?" she said to herself as much as to her sister. "I agreed. We start on Monday. He plans to meet me at the garden. It's distribution day, so he'll be working with the volunteers."

"Then do what you need to do, but nothing more. However, you'll need to tell Drew about your anxiety. He can help you through this. I trust Drew enough, but not where your heart is concerned. Keep that kind, sensitive organ of yours tucked away. If he can't see it, he won't want it. And maybe you should buy an outfit from one of your homeless friends. Better yet, I can design you something for your dates that will turn him away."

Julia chuckled. "You know I'm going to be on television, and the point is to win people over, point them to the nonprofit and what the garden is doing for the community. Besides, you don't want negative reviews on your designs in front of hundreds of people."

Kaylie leaned back in her chair. "Good point. I'll have to make you something unforgettable."

"Would you like a name drop during dinner?"

"I wouldn't be opposed." She laughed. "This is crazy. The entire thing is nuts, but no matter what happens, know I'm here and praying for you. Because it's obvious our waitress couldn't find any *good judgment* back there either."

Julia grinned and shook her head at her sister. She was something, but she was also right. Julia needed to keep praying. She'd find peace with the situation one way or another, even if she needed to guard her heart where Andrew was concerned. He broke it once. She couldn't allow him to do it again, no matter how right his touch felt.

Five

Andrew had parked two blocks away from the garden, and now he was hurrying to make his meeting time with Julia. He had been early, but as he'd circled several blocks looking for a parking spot, he'd witnessed something he hadn't seen before: a horde of people stretched in long lines along the city sidewalks, waiting for access to a garden. It looked more like a concert line for a top billboard performer than a food line. There were more hungry people than one would think in this town.

Nearing the line, he smiled. "Excuse me. May I get by?"

The people standing around gave him the eye. One lady planted a hand on her hip, and he had the feeling she was going to defend her spot at all costs.

"I'm here to help," he hurried to add. "A volunteer."

With the lady's hand still firmly planted, she stepped aside and waved at the man next to her wearing a faded Dallas Cowboys t-shirt. "Hank, get out of the man's way."

The man mumbled something under his breath but did as he was told.

"Thank you," Andrew said to the couple. He found Julia speaking with a group and headed toward them. He edged in on the gathering and joined the conversation.

"Yes, it seems our lines are growing," she was saying. "Please plan to stay if you can until everyone has been served or we run out of food. You know what to do, so let's get started." She noticed him then, and her eyes brightened. "Andrew, you made it."

"Why wouldn't I? It's our first official date together." And just like that, her eyes dimmed, and she looked away. How could he be so careless with his words? He'd fix this between them somehow. "So, tell me, how do you sift through those in need and those who are truly homeless?"

She brought her gaze back to him. "We don't. I wish there was an exact science, but one of the ways we try to ensure the best possible outcome is that we've built relationships with other nonprofits that share our desire to help people." Julia led him over to several tables and began stuffing bags with soap and shampoo. He did the same. The bags already contained toothbrushes and toothpaste. "They help us get the word out to low-income families, the military and their families, and to senior citizens. I provide a form with a few questions, like their first and last name, their gender, age, ethnicity, and zip code. Then the organizations email me the list of people who qualify, and when they arrive, volunteers help them find their names on two bags, one with the goodies we're packing and one with food. They sign that they received the food and other goodies that businesses have donated for the cause.

Andrew nodded to where two lines ended at different tables. "But there's two lines."

"The line on the left is for those who signed up. The people on the right are those who came off the streets. They're waiting to see if we have anything left over. It's the reason I want another garden. By asking for their zip codes, I've learned that we're serving people from surrounding counties, thirteen people from outside our county in fact. We need more land to grow. When the garden is producing, and we're fully staffed with paid workers and volunteers, we'll do this once every week."

"That's a lot of people." Andrew trained his attention to the flurry of activity, the people waiting in lines, those serving, the beauty of the community coming together. "We need cameras here." He withdrew his phone from his pocket, slid the screen open, and dialed. His friend answered on the second ring. "Hey, Joy, I need your help. Can you make it down to the city garden under the downtown bridge, next to the park? I'm volunteering at the garden, and I need some eyes down here for people to know what's going on. It's incredible."

"Sure. I'm still in the area. I finished my assignment and was heading to grab some coffee before driving back. I'll swing by first."

"Perfect. See you then. And thanks." He ended the call with a smile. "We're going to make this happen, Juls. You'll see."

She cleared her throat and glanced away. "I hate to cut this short, but I had you working with someone today. See the college student with the auburn hair? Her name is Angie, and next to her is Erralee. She's the one with dark hair. She's a high school student needing some volunteer hours. Head over to them, introduce yourself, and they'll tell you what to do next."

Why did he feel like he was being sent to the corner? Had he offended Julia? She was sending him away and avoiding looking at him. Whatever he'd done, he had to break the ice. "When Joy arrives, I'll introduce you." He bowed gallantly. "Until then, I'm at your service." When he straightened, she was fighting a smile. He winked, then headed to where she directed, glad the ice between them was beginning to melt.

Contentment settled over Julia as she thought about her day, even though her limbs were sore, her bones weary, and her mind exhausted. A smile lingered on her lips. The day's events had been successful in many ways, and she couldn't begin to thank Andrew enough for sending Joy over to take pictures. Joy had sent them to her in an email before Julia had even gotten home. Another email was sent to their radio station, then it was sent to one of their affiliate newspapers to be printed in Thursday's "What's Happening Around Town" column. Andrew was doing what he'd promised.

She thought back to the moment before she sent him away to work with Angie and Erralee. She hadn't meant to be abrupt, but the way he called her by his nickname for her, like he had so long ago on her doorstep... There was too much heartache in the past. It was as if he'd sealed her fate to misery as she thought of him over the years. And today, when he'd jumped in to help, to hear the excitement in his voice, to see her own passion in his eyes, she'd had to send him away.

Her desire to find a man who loved serving others as much as she did had never lessened over the years. She still believed there was someone out there, but seeing Andrew today, hearing what he called her, her heart gave a thud so violent within her chest, she'd forgotten to breathe.

Six

Andrew was due to arrive at Amore Restaurant at any moment, but the wait was agonizing. Julia sat in her idling parked car, hands trembling in her lap. Through the rearview mirror, she observed the camera crew in the distance, gathering for what looked like a meeting.

There were so few words that described how Julia felt over her predicament. Not only this date with Andrew, but the cameras and her need to get through the next hour. And against her every fear, the hope that somehow she'd show Andrew how she truly felt for him in the process without speaking a word.

It had been days since they'd seen each other, though he'd texted during the week, a "good morning" or "good night," and her response was always brief. She'd been trying to suppress the emotions dragging her back to their past only to be faced with the reality her heart hadn't changed. The truth was freeing, but she didn't trust him enough not to walk away from her a second time.

Andrew pulled into the parking lot and parked further from where the camera crew's meeting had begun, but closer to where she parked. Julia had to intercept him, to tell him she wasn't sure she could do this.

She grabbed her cell and began to text when he climbed from his car. He headed in her general direction. Had he seen her car? He was weaving his way through the parking lot and would soon walk behind her vehicle. With the car still on, she put it in reverse and rolled down the window, stopping him.

A smile lifted his mouth. "Hello," he said, through the open window.

"Get in."

His smile widened, and he had the nerve to wink before opening the car door and sliding into the passenger seat. As the window rose, he asked, "Are you kidnapping me?"

He thought she was kidding, but he was sadly mistaken. "Yes." She turned the wheel and drove out of the parking lot.

"You're being serious." He latched his seat belt and shifted to face her.

"I'll take you wherever you want to go."

"As tempting as that is, and I do mean tempting, we need to go back. And when I say *we* that means you and I."

"Not exactly. You know I can hire someone to play as my double. While I won't be falling from the twentieth floor, they can still save me from a death of humiliation. I do have the means, and it would be well worth the cost."

"This is really bothering you?"

"Were you not listening to me earlier when I said I couldn't do this?"

"I did, but I thought . . . It doesn't matter what I thought."

"What did you think?"

"I thought you were talking about going on a date with me."

Julia took a long breath and slowed the car, then pulled into a car dealership and found a parking spot near the entrance. She turned off the engine and met the worry in his gaze. "This fear I'm feeling has nothing to do with you or our past."

Knowing it was better to get it over with, she plunged

into her story. "My sister and I used to model in Italy when we lived there." Her voice fell away, and she felt him move closer, but she continued, "We were discovered by a booking agent walking down the street with our parents. He wanted us both, but my parents felt I was too young to be separated from Kaylie, so they made previsions that Kaylie and I would stay together. I did fine in simple photoshoots. The room was full of people, but it was really the photographer and three of his assistants that had eyes on what was going on. My sister was the real beauty, so it took the pressure off, and she was always by my side. With her being four years older, she was the security my parents wanted, and she became the security I needed." She paused. "This next part . . . I should be over it now, but it changed me."

He held out his palm to her. "You're losing blood flow in your hand with that death grip on the steering wheel."

A glimpse at her fingers showed they'd turned white.

"Come on." He ran the hand he offered down her forearm to her fingers, coaxing her palm into his. "Good. Now continue."

His hand was firm against hers, strong, she realized, and when he ran a gentle thumb across her knuckles, she inhaled a calming breath.

"It was our first runway show, and I was nervous. I understood Kaylie and I wouldn't be together for some time, but once it was my turn, I couldn't do it. The next thing I remember, I'm on the runway, frozen in place in front of cameras and hundreds of people." A tremor went through her, and she tightened her hold on his hand.

"It's okay."

"I had an anxiety attack. My heart was racing so fast. I didn't know what it was at the time, but I couldn't breathe. I couldn't move. Someone must have told Kaylie because she was the one who helped me from the stage. I couldn't voice what had happened, but she wouldn't leave my side. The next day, my parents began preparations to leave and fly us back to the States. Kaylie was nineteen at the time and stayed behind to find another modeling job, but she was tainted because of me, and it ultimately shut the door for her designing career. She does some work for a local brand in town, but things changed after that. For all of us."

"How old were you?"

"Fifteen."

"I'm sorry, Julia. I hope you don't mind me asking, but do you still have anxiety attacks?"

She hated to admit it. What would he think of her? "I do, especially when I find myself in the public eye." When he said nothing, she released his hand. "I should take you back. I'll plead innocent to your kidnapping charge. I don't look good in orange, and I'm not going to jail for anyone." A knock on the window jolted Julia, and she yelped.

A well-dressed man stood at the passenger side door.

Andrew rolled down the window. "Sorry, we needed a place to talk. We'll get out of your hair."

The man's gaze fell to Julia. He strolled over to her side of the car, and she rolled down her window. "Is everything all right?" he asked, looking her directly in the eye.

Julia glanced at his name badge. "It is." She gave him a grateful smile. "Thank you for checking, Alex."

"Actually, she's the one who kidnapped me," Andrew stated with a teasing glint in his eyes.

She smiled at him. "He wishes."

Alex chuckled. "If either of you need another car to talk in, I can help you find just the right vehicle."

"Thanks, Alex. We will." Andrew gave a quick wave as Julia rolled up their windows. "Nice guy."

She pulled out of the parking lot and headed back toward Amore Restaurant. "What do we do now about your boss? I'm sure he's tried to reach you."

"I've had a few missed calls and texts since we left." He withdrew his cell from his pocket and looked at the screen. "You're right. Let me call him." Andrew dialed, and the ring was loud enough for her to hear. "Michael—"

"Where are you! I have a crew here waiting, and you are nowhere to be seen."

Andrew looked to Julia. "There's been a change of plans. She doesn't feel well tonight and couldn't make it."

"Then why am I hearing about this now? You know time is money. Where are you?"

"Heading your way."

"Good, because we need to talk about the stunt you pulled the other day. You were supposed to be with your first kiss, not downtown volunteering at the gardens."

She whispered, "Tell Michael I was there at the garden too, and it was one of our dates. I chose. That should satisfy him. You can tell him you're with me now too. I don't mind. Really. I have to make this up to you somehow."

"Who's with you, Drew? Don't tell me you're on a different date than the one you're supposed to be on."

Andrew shook his head. "Michael, it's fine. I'm with Julia."

"What? Then when you get here, we have some things to discuss, and I want to meet her." He hung up.

Andrew pocketed his phone. "I'm thirty-eight and feel like I'm going to the principal's office for fighting."

"Sounds like you know the experience."

His lazy smile returned. "A time or two. What was I to do to keep myself busy when the girl I used to chase moved away?"

They pulled into the restaurant's parking lot, and the

person Julia assumed was Michael was staring them down as she parked. "Ready, hooligan?"

"As long as you have my boxing gloves." He got out of the car and came around to her side and held the door.

She got out, and seeing Michael striding toward them, she leaned back against Andrew. "You can tell him the truth, that I kidnapped you."

He leaned closer to her ear. "I can see it now: Drew Larsen, radio show host, is kidnapped by his first kiss in an act of passion. You don't know Michael. He might use it for ratings."

He closed the door, and she smiled. "I've been warned. Thank you, *Drew*."

She called him *Drew*. Even though she did so to tease him, he caught Michael watching, and said nothing. The use of his radio name felt impersonal, and after what she'd shared, he didn't much care for it, but he understood as Michael continued to stare between them, then directly at her. Andrew had never mentioned who Julia truly was to him or that she'd once owned Morgan Tech, but it wouldn't be long until he discovered her identity. Andrew had hoped for that to happen later rather than sooner so Michael wouldn't push their relationship further than meeting twice a week.

"Ms. Julia, I take it."

"Yes, Julia Morgan." She held out her hand. "And you are?"

Michael looked to him and then back at Julia and took her hand. "Michael Daniels. I'm the station manager."

"Of course." Julia released his hand and smiled like she was pleased to meet him. "Drew has told me such wonderful things about you and your station. And I can't tell you how grateful I am you were able to highlight the garden and the great work they do for our community. Have you been down there yourself?"

"No, I can't say as I have." Michael's eyes narrowed, then widened. Andrew was sure Michael now knew the truth.

"I know for a fact that the garden will be distributing food to the community again next week. Drew and I plan to be there. You should join us. It will be worth your time, and you'll have an experience like no other."

"I'll think on it, Ms. Morgan." Michael stood taller, rubbing his unshaven face. "Now, about tonight's date. Are you sure you're not feeling well enough? Drew made it sound like you needed to cancel."

"Since my drive, I do feel a little better, but . . ."

"How about we make a few adjustments?" Andrew said. "Maybe they can get footage of us going into Amore Restaurant, a few minutes inside, but just general wide shots. Photos will be fine as well. Will that work?"

Julia released a large exhale. "Thank you for understanding. Yes, that will work."

Michael eyed him. "It wasn't what I had in mind, but I suppose. Ms. Morgan, how did you meet Drew?"

"Did he not tell you? He was my first kiss." Julia looked at Andrew, then back at Michael. "Excuse me, gentlemen, I left something in the car. I'll be right back."

Michael waited until Julia was out of earshot before saying, "*She* was your first kiss, and you didn't bother to tell me? She's a corporate mogul! This is a gold mine, Drew."

Andrew faced Michael, his defenses rising. "I'm not going to push her into doing something she's not comfortable with, because if I do, she'll walk, and I can't let that happen. We both can't let that happen."

Michael gave him a look he couldn't read and glanced in

the direction Julia had gone. "Then you have your work cut out for you. You have two people to make happy. If one walks, so does the other."

The sun had already set and the stars were shining bright as Andrew strolled at Julia's side to her car. Andrew was glad Michael had kept his word, but he was still surprised when the cameras left shortly before they finished dinner. Once Andrew realized they'd have time alone, he'd ordered her favorite dessert—chocolate cheesecake—on Michael. "Thank you for what you did tonight."

She chuckled lightly. "You're welcome, but I'm glad that's done."

He placed a hand over his heart. "You wound me. I haven't been on a date in years, and now I can guess why. It's the company."

Her laugh brought a grin to his lips. She unlocked the car door, then swung her purse onto the passenger seat. "It had nothing to do with you, and you know it." She turned to him, the smile he'd placed on her lips still there.

"Julia, before you go, I wanted to tell you how much I appreciate you sharing with me this afternoon. It meant a lot, still means a lot. I'm here for you. I'll help you anyway I can, even if I have to manage Michael, I'd do it for you."

"Your boss doesn't seem like such a bad guy."

"Yeah, he's a nice guy underneath all that gruff, but now that he knows who you are, I can guarantee more cameras, and he'll try to force my hand."

"I had a feeling about the cameras. What do you think he'll do?"

"Not sure, but we need to plan our weeks, dates, and times as soon as possible. I'd say by Monday at least."

"Then we'll do it. We can schedule everything."

"Are you free tomorrow or Sunday?"

"Text me and I'll see how the weekend is going." A wistful look shone in her gaze. "I have a standing engagement tomorrow afternoon."

He hesitated. Of course, she'd have a standing engagement. A *real* date. He fought his next words to be casual, undetached. "Sure. Well, I should let you go. I'll text you." He held the car door for her, and after she slid in, closed it, and waved goodbye as she drove off.

Later that night, Andrew lay in bed, replaying his day with Julia and all she had shared. He wanted her to know he'd be there for her if she ever needed him, but he'd told her that once before and failed her. He'd never make that same mistake twice, but how could she believe him?

Andrew wasn't sure of his next steps, though he was certain of one thing, he had to prove himself to Juls. That he was indeed the man she'd believed him to be all those years ago. If it hadn't been for her father, things would have been different. He stopped himself from continuing down that thought process again and began to pray.

"Lord, I didn't know how to handle the situation in the past, and I still don't, but there's no one standing in my way this time. If this is Your will, I pray she forgives me for walking away, that she'll continue to open herself up toward me, and for her heart to feel safe. Amen."

With a sense of courage, Andrew nabbed his cell from the nightstand and texted her.

I had a nice time today.

To his surprise, a quote bubble popped up on his phone screen, showing she was texting back. Was she on her phone?

Waiting for him to text? It was an absurd thought, but he could wish.

I did too. Thank you for listening.

Anytime.

Goodnight, Andrew.

Nite Juls.

Seven

Julia wore a pink hat and a flowered dress she'd found at the thrift store. She tugged at the oversized waist, thankful for the gazebo's fan above their heads. It was fall, but with the warmer-than-average week they were having, she was thankful for the small things. She leaned over to pour tea into her niece's teacup. "Stacey, would you care for some sugar?"

Her six-year-old niece lifted her chin in a proud look, and her soft words squeaked through her lips. "It's English Rose, is it not? I can't drink my tea if it's not."

Julia continued to pour tea for their "guests"—Mr. Tiger, Mrs. Bear, and Mr. Astronaut—as they sat patiently waiting. "Do you require sugar as well?"

Stacey took a sip from her cup before announcing that everyone needed sugar, or why else would they drink tea?

Biting her lip to keep from laughing, Julia spooned a teaspoon of sugar into their cups before sitting next to Stacey and their guests. Julia wasn't sure where Stacey got the idea they were only allowed to be aristocrats during tea, but she couldn't tell her otherwise. Julia supposed that's the way things were as the youngest of five. Kaylie's children were like her own since she was nearing forty and had never married. She thought of Andrew then and how she'd fallen hard for a boy with big dreams, dreams that hadn't included her.

"Dear, did you hear me?" Stacey broke through Julia's

thoughts, and she noticed for the first time that her niece's feathered hat rested on her plate, covering her frosted cookie. Plastic pink beads that had once hung around Stacy's neck now rolled around the patio table. Her bottom lip trembled.

"Oh, forgive me, Niece. I lost concentration. We'll make another necklace." She bent to collect the beads as Andrew walked across the yard toward their makeshift tea party. She nabbed a couple more beads and sat up. "Is it two already?"

"A few minutes before. So, this is your standing engagement? I do enjoy a good tea party. May I join you?"

Stacey looked him up and down as he stepped into the gazebo. "And who are you?"

"An old friend of Julia's."

Her niece's gaze swung to Julia as if to make certain he spoke the truth. Julia gave her a nod. "Lady Julia, he doesn't look old."

She smiled, fighting back a foreign fluttering within her stomach. "No, dear, he does not. May he join us?"

"He must bow first." She turned to him and tilted her head.

Andrew's lips tightened against a smile. "Where are my manners." He gave a deep bow. Julia turned away quickly to keep from laughing and continued to collect the remaining beads. Out of the corner of her eye, she watched as Andrew lifted Mr. Bear from his chair and took his place, setting him on his knee. It was strange, but it seemed natural for the small bear to be propped up on his knee, the way he was smiling at Stacey, as if he was truly enjoying himself.

After securing the last bead, Julia lifted the tea pot. "Sir Andrew, would you care for some tea?"

"Tea will be lovely, Lady Julia. And while I cannot address your niece since we've not been properly introduced, I must say, she is a fine young lady, and I see the resemblance."

"Then let me introduce you. Lady Stacey, this is my dearest friend, Sir Andrew. Sir Andrew, my sister's youngest daughter, Lady Stacey." She handed Sir Andrew his tea.

Stacey gave him a wide smile. "Thank you for joining us."

Kaylie appeared from the house at that moment and took in the scene. Her sister had known Andrew was coming—it had been her idea they'd meet here, probably to keep an eye on them. But now Julia almost regretted it, what with the steel look in her sister's gaze. Hopefully Andrew hadn't noticed. She'd talk with her later.

"Kaylie," Julia said, motioning toward Andrew. "I take it you've met?"

"We did. It's nice to put a face with the voice," her sister said, going around the table to where her daughter sat. "Lady Stacey, your aunt has a guest. I request your presence in the library."

Her niece's brown eyes, much like her own, widened, then pleaded for her to stay. "Mommy?"

"Sorry, Honey. Grab Mr. Bear, Mr. Tiger, and your brother's astronaut. If he finds it out here, he wouldn't be too happy."

She huffed and grabbed the astronaut and tiger. "Thank you for visiting, Sir Andrew. Mr. Bear is required in the library. I shall take him there personally." She leaned into Andrew. "Before mother has the vapers." She straightened, curtsied, then accepted Mr. Bear from Andrew before running toward the house. Kaylie followed.

"She has the best imagination." Julia stood and pointed toward his cup. "Don't forget to drink your tea." She began stacking the dishes.

He stood quickly, reaching out to help her. "Let me take those into the house for you."

"I got it. Thank you, though. I'll be back in a minute." Julia walked to the house and caught her sister looking out the kitchen window before she faded from view. "Kaylie," she called once she entered, and her sister turned from the pantry. "I didn't realize I had a spy on my hands."

"I wasn't spying. Not really." She set a box of noodles on the counter.

"Then what do you call it?"

She lowered her voice. "A caring sister. I don't want you to get hurt."

"I won't."

"And how can you be so sure?" Kaylie's gaze sought hers, concern reflected from her eyes straight to Julia's heart. She didn't know how to respond, really. She was doing this in hopes of garnishing more publicity for her garden, not to fall for Andrew again. Her heart squeezed within her chest at the secret she'd tried to hide over the years, even from herself. But deep within her, she knew the answer, and as if her sister could read her thoughts, she gave her a knowing frown.

"It will work itself out. You'll see." Julia strolled to the living room and collected her calendar from the desk. She ignored her sister as she walked back out to where Andrew waited.

Andrew waited for Julia to return, but he couldn't help his need to pace. After his second pass of the bird bath, he looked to the house. Julia was walking toward him with a bag in her hands. Too much was riding on their time together, and he didn't know if he was coming or going. He wanted to please Julia and make her feel comfortable, but he was afraid he'd boxed himself in a corner where Michael was concerned. Would he be pleased with their plans, or would he nix them as soon as he heard?

He paused his pacing at Julia's approach. The brown curls falling from her pink, brimmed hat did nothing to distract from her beauty, and the way her eyes shone when she looked at him . . . He smiled.

"What?" she asked, her eyes growing wide. "I guess I should have changed. We dress up for teatime."

"I know my grandmother would have loved your dress. She's partial to flowers too."

She touched the brim of her hat and chuckled. She took it off and began patting her hair. "I'm sure I'm a mess."

"On the contrary," he said, wanting to tell her how beautiful she was. How her eyes mesmerized him, and her sun-kissed skin drew him to see if it was really as soft as he remembered. He pulled his gaze away and bowed. "Lady Julia, where do you care to sit?"

She gave him a soft smile. "Now that Lady Stacey is with her mother, governess, and nurse maid, all in one, I think we can resume our natural familiarity. Wouldn't you agree, Sir Andrew?" She retook her seat at the table, so he did the same, sitting across from her, where Mr. Bear had been and his teacup still sat.

"And what familiarity are you speaking of?" he asked. Julia's gaze jumped to him, and a worried expression filtered across her features, making Andrew regret his words.

Julia quickly hunted through her bag and, at finding her calendar, opened it to the month of November. Unclasping her pen from one of its pages, she began writing. "One week down, three more to go."

Three? He took out his phone and checked the calendar. She was correct, and somehow, he knew the rest of their time together would slip through his fingers. He wanted Julia in his life again, and if the only way to move forward was to revisit the past, he'd find a way. "So, Mondays are garden days. What would you care to do on Fridays?"

She shrugged. "It's up to you."

Andrew had an idea, but would she go along with it?

"What?" She eyed him, her face tilting slightly at an angle. "You look suspicious over there."

"Where?" He pretended ignorance, frowning for effect. "Here?" he pointed to his seat, not two feet away from her. "I have no idea what you mean."

"Out with it."

He wanted more time with Julia, and he had an idea just how to do it. "We'll go Christmas shopping."

Eight

"You were being serious on Saturday?" Julia chuckled under her breath, but Andrew still heard it, and he loved the sound.

He wiped the sweat from his face with a towel and raised a brow. "Are you one of those people who won't shop for Christmas until Thanksgiving is over?"

"No." She pulled her gardening gloves off and stuffed them in the back pocket of her jeans. "But it seems funny hearing you mention shopping for tree decorations." She turned and gazed out at their newly planted rows of Swiss chard lettuce, before looking in the camera crew's direction.

"What are you trying to say, *Lady Julia*?" He tried to distract her.

She smiled at him then and shook her head. "You surprise me is all. Not only do you know how to play pretend, plow ground, and plant, but you also don't like to wait for the last minute to shop for Christmas."

"Does that mean we're on for Friday? I know it's a different type of date, but it might help you relax if the cameras aren't solely focused on you the entire time."

"It sounds like fun, and you're right, of course."

"Great, I'll pick you up about five." He heard Michael calling, but he ignored him, wanting to set his plans with Julia before Michael interrupted. "We can get a bite to eat first, then shop. I'll take you to one of my favorite places."

"Where are you taking me?" Her smile faded as she looked over her shoulder.

"You'll find out." He followed her gaze, and at seeing the camera crew packing up and Michael heading their way, his body tensed. He didn't like the look on Michael's face.

"Andrew and Julia," Michael said as he reached them. "We need to talk. Starting today, we'll be promoting 'My First Kiss' heavily with snippets from the time you spent together last week. This will lead listeners and the other outlets who follow along into Friday, for our first live broadcast. This will set the stage for the next four weeks—"

"Four weeks?" Julia interrupted. "You mean three, since there are only three weeks left."

"True, there are only three *full* weeks remaining, but there are several other days that need to be accounted for." Michael turned to him, arms folding against his chest. "It was my understanding this was for the entire month. As to our agreement."

Andrew opened his mouth, though he didn't know what to say, but Julia spoke up. "Drew did say a month, but I missed his meaning. Then to clarify, our agreement ends on the last day of November?"

"With a bang. I'd like for us to sit down this week and plan your outings."

"Actually." Andrew nodded to Julia. "We've already planned the month. I'd be happy to go over the calendar with you."

Michael ran a hand down the scruff of his jaw and looked toward the garden. Julia must have felt his aggravation as clearly as he did because she pulled her gloves from her back pocket and slipped them on. "Well, gentlemen, I have a couple of things to do before I can head out, so I'll leave you both to it. Michael, good to see you." She turned to Andrew with a secretive smile. "Andrew."

"I'll call you."

Julia nodded, then headed toward the newly planted

vegetables. Yesterday, when she discovered a mom-and-pop greenhouse with container-grown crops, she'd texted him to see if he would help her plant their own. It made her happy, so of course he agreed. She was stretching the last planting season of the year, but he told her there was nothing to lose.

"It seems things are progressing nicely."

Andrew forced his gaze from Julia to his boss. "What is?"

"Your time with Julia."

"I'm not sure what you're getting at." But Andrew had a gut feeling he knew where Michael's thoughts had taken him.

"If you say so, *Andrew*. I've never heard anyone call you anything besides *Drew*. She tries, but she slips from time to time."

"We knew each other before Drew was even a thing. It means nothing to her. What you see between us is friendship, two friends helping each other out. I offered her a business proposition, and she accepted."

"Really? Tell me about this business arrangement."

Andrew realized a little too late what he'd given away. Leverage. And there was no going back. "She's helping me because she needs more eyes on her garden project. She tried to expand into the next county, but it was rejected. She believes if she can inform more people about the garden's outreach and how it's helping the community, it will make a difference."

"I think I recall something about this. She wants two blocks."

"Yes."

"She has skin in the game." His gaze drifted to where Julia was speaking with a group of volunteers. "She served a hundred and ninety-seven people today. I counted. And the amount of food, plus the donated items from surrounding businesses, she knows how to rally people for a cause."

Michael went silent, and Andrew did as well to let the man think. There was no doubt it would affect not only Julia, but him. "I'll make it happen," Michael blurted.

He frowned. "Make what happen?"

"I'll give Julia what she's after."

The hairs at the back of Andrew's neck stood on end. What was Michael after? Whatever it was, Andrew had a feeling he wasn't going to like it. "I'm not sure I care where this might be going."

"All you have to do is play your cards right, then everything will work out as it should."

"What does that mean?"

"You need to set up a time for the three of us to meet. And tomorrow, you're going to pitch and sell this series to your listeners. In the morning, I'll have a printout on your desk of the different station channels, TV channel, blogs, websites, and podcasts that have agreed to host your dates with Julia."

"Sounds good, but you need to know something. Julia doesn't like cameras. She freezes up—"

"Then be aware that wherever you go, the cameras will be rolling, but I'm fine with whatever activities you've set up for your dates," Michael interrupted. "Well, except for the thirtieth, since it seems it was overlooked."

Andrew opened his mouth to object, but Michael's lifted hand silenced his words. Michael smirked. "I have an evening to plan. A grand finale if you will. You can leave this one up to me." Michael's phone chimed. He took his cell from his pants pocket and scanned the screen. "I've gotta go, but remember," he said without meeting his gaze, "the list of places sharing your dates will be on your desk. Make certain to share them with your listeners." Michael hurried off in the direction the camera crew was heading, leaving Andrew to wonder what was behind Michael's smirk, and what his plans for the last night he and Julia would be together were.

Julia was still hesitant about Andrew picking her up like it was a real date. She didn't want to disillusion herself where Andrew was concerned, because he was a friendly type of guy. She didn't want to believe their time together meant more to him than the bargain they made to help each other.

She couldn't stop thinking about her sister and their conversation at the restaurant. What Kaylie told her was true, every word of it, but Julia's heart didn't want to be tucked away so he couldn't find it. Just the opposite. She wanted him to notice her, who she was inside and out. When they were together, her heart seemed to sing a new song, shouting its rhythm to the tips of her toes. She loved being with him and how he made her smile. The problem was, she wasn't a teenager any longer, but a grown woman afraid of falling for her high school sweetheart all over again. She didn't know what the next few weeks would hold, but she did know who would capitalize on those feelings if he found out. Michael. He was a shrewd man, and the only way to protect herself was to control the narrative. If she didn't, she'd find herself stepping back into her fifteen-year-old shoes, faced with cameras, frozen, and desperate for breath. While everyone watched.

Nine

Andrew came back from commercial with Michael's list in hand. "I have a special surprise for you, my wonderful listeners. Because of your overwhelming support sharing your first kiss stories, the station has decided for me to reconnect with my first kiss."

A red light flashed, and the entire caller board lit in his peripheral. He chuckled. "I see by the calls coming in you're excited. There's more news, but I'll take a couple of callers. You're on the air."

"Drew, this is Tamika. Do you care to share your first kiss's name now that you'll be seeing her again after all these years?"

"Tamika, as a surprise, we actually met last week. And about her name, I'll give you her first, it's Julia."

"You met last week, and we're just hearing about this! And we weren't invited? Details!"

"We need some secrets, Tamika, but keep listening because it only gets better. If you visit our website, you'll find pictures and videos of our time together. There's even a special surprise for you, special content that can only be found at our website. Go check it out. Thanks for calling." Andrew tried to play off his words in a casual tone, but would people really try to join them once they knew of their dates? Tamika acted like she would.

Michael came into view through the studio window and gave him a nod.

"Speaking of secrets, I want my listeners to be the first to hear the news that Julia and I have agreed to meet twice a week for the rest of the month. Mondays we'll be at the All-Roads Garden downtown serving the community, and Fridays are our date nights."

He pressed one of the call buttons. "Caller, you're on the air."

"There's nothing there," a woman's voice shrieked over the line. "I'm at the website, and there's nothing there."

Michael held up a piece of paper with thick blue marker written across the page. He read it. "I've just learned that after my show is over, a new link, called *Drew and Julia*, will be live."

"Did you kiss?" she asked.

Andrew grinned, thankful the listeners couldn't see, but he'd forgotten about Michael. That sly look of his was back, and Andrew didn't care for it. "No, we didn't, but we had a great time catching up."

"Thanks for calling. It seems my time is coming to a close. Remember to join us each week on our website." He promoted each affiliate Michael had listed and their sister station ARP, where their dates would be live streamed.

"Until tomorrow, have a great day." He set a song to play and took off his headset. Michael met him at the booth and held the door open for him to exit. "This is becoming a habit. Did you want to see me?"

They began walking down the hall.

"What are your plans for Friday?"

"I'm taking her for a bite to eat before heading to buy the station's ornaments."

"Drew, are you trying to scare her off? Is that the best you have after not seeing this woman for years?"

"We're not really dating, Michael, and if we were, I wouldn't change much. Julia is a down-to-earth girl and has always been. Money hasn't changed her, and I won't act like it has."

"Women like romance."

"Despite what you might think, I care about Julia, and I don't plan to lead her on for weeks and then walk away." But isn't that what Julia thought he did after high school? Regardless of what her father had insisted, Andrew should have at least spoken to her, explained why he was walking away. Her hurt was still evident from time to time, and he felt an invisible wedge between them. He wanted to remove it, but he didn't know how. "I hurt her once, Michael. I won't do it again. Not even for this job."

"You'd give it all up for her?" Michael asked as they reached the elevators.

He was saved from answering when the elevator doors opened, and Julia walked out. At spotting her, he grinned. "Fancy meeting you here."

She returned his smile, then smiled at Michael. "I was in the neighborhood. I hope I'm not intruding."

"Not at all," Michael said. "I'll leave you two so you can talk. Drew, I'll see you in an hour." Michael strolled away, leaving them standing in front of the elevators.

"What brings you by?" he asked.

Her smile slipped. "Can we speak privately?"

"I was just heading out for a bite to eat. We can walk and talk. I need to be back for a meeting in an hour." He pushed the elevator button.

"It's not about us, is it?"

"Not exactly." The elevator doors opened, and they entered. Andrew pushed the lobby button. "I'm officially in the running against two other people for the morning host spot. The station heads planned another round of interview questions on how to handle callers. Thankfully, there hasn't been a caller I didn't know how to respond to." The doors slid open, and Andrew followed Julia out of the elevators.

"Well congratulations. I hope everything goes well."

"I'm sure it will. Now tell me, why did you come all this way when you could have called?"

"I really was in the neighborhood. I thought it would be easier to tell you in person since it was on my mind."

"Tell me what?" He held the door open for her, and they started down the sidewalk.

"I won't be able to make the garden on Monday. I hope it won't be a problem."

"It's nothing serious, is it?"

She shook her head. "No. I have a senior volunteer who needs a ride to dialysis once a month, but she asked if I was free to take her today and on Monday. That's where I've been, at the hospital. I have a few hours to waste so I thought I'd stop by to tell you."

"I'm glad you did. I only wish I had more time." He pointed to a food truck a few feet away. "Interested in a hot dog or a corn dog?"

"Lunch of champions, I see. Sure, I'll take a corn dog."

Andrew ordered, and after being handed their meal, they grabbed their condiments. He pointed to a bench. "Will this work?"

"Perfect," she said, leading the way. "What do you think Michael will say?"

Andrew waited for her as she lowered to the bench before he sat. He handed her the corn dog and sweet tea. "I'm sure it will be fine." He took a bite and wiped his mouth with a napkin, wondering if Michael would be okay with the change as he'd hoped. "If I have enough time before the meeting, I'll mention it to him. If not, I'll wait until after." He glanced at his watch and caught a spot of mustard at the corner of Julia's mouth. He grinned to himself and focused on the watch. He needed to return to the office, but as he looked back at Julia, where the mustard still lingered, his eyes trailed to the heart-shaped freckle on her jawline. More times than he cared to remember, he imagined running his thumb across her jawline and over the heart shape. The impulse to do just that raised his pulse, and when he caught Julia watching him, he couldn't turn away. Instead, he hesitantly met her gaze, afraid she'd leave him where he sat, but she didn't move. His mind went blank.

"You remembered my freckle. You mentioned it on the radio."

"How could I forget? Even your love of sweet tea, and mustard with your corn dogs, hasn't been forgotten." He leaned over and ran a thumb at the corner of her mouth, wiping at the mustard. "Julia," he whispered her name. There was too much to say, but he didn't have time, especially not here in front of the food truck. He leaned away. "I should go if I want to talk with Michael before the meeting."

She nodded. "Let me know what he says."

He stood, enjoying the view of her and the lingering mustard at her mouth. He nodded and handed her a napkin. "You might need this."

She smiled at him. "Thank you."

He hurried back to the station, unable to believe what he'd done, touching her like he had. The thing was, she didn't seem to mind. There lay the problem. If she had, he'd know where he stood, but this, he wasn't sure how to proceed.

Andrew saw Michael stepping off the elevator shortly after him. "I need a few minutes before the meeting."

"You're in luck, we have nine. Does this have to do with Julia's visit?"

"She isn't going to be at the garden on Monday. It seems she drives one of the volunteers to dialysis."

"I see. Did you reschedule?"

"I didn't think it necessary."

"Drew, I'm surprised at you. With everything that's on the line . . . Make no mistake, I want it rescheduled. Text me the details when you know them." He pulled his cell from his pocket. "Five minutes. Don't be late."

Andrew took a fortifying breath, pushed back the thoughts of Julia, and followed Michael into the conference room.

Ten

Julia stood in front of her mirror for a final glance. The pleated sunflower printed blouse her sister made for her looked great with her dark jeans and brown boots. Of course, she wanted to look nice on camera, but she couldn't deceive herself into thinking that's all it was, not anymore. Yes, at first, she wanted Andrew to notice her, but if yesterday was any indication, he had, but it wasn't enough. She wasn't sure how it happened. It was as if being in his presence breathed new life into the dormant dream she'd carried of them all these years ago, buried deep beneath the hurt he'd left behind. Yet, here she was, fighting this longing for him, realizing a little too late that she'd already given her heart away. What would he do with it once he realized it as well? Would he walk away from her again?

Fear was the reason she wouldn't breathe a word of how she felt, not yet. She needed more time to reassure herself the risk was worth taking, especially with Michael hovering around. Even with her hesitation, she noticed Andrew seemed to have a closer relationship with the Lord than before, how his care for her was real. Though he never said the words out loud, she felt them in his nightly texts, and in the way he listened and took her words to heart, especially with helping her handle the pressures she felt with his boss and the cameras.

A small sigh of contentment left her lungs. Though they hadn't spoken since last night, she had listened to Andrew's show today, and calls filled the air waves more than they normally did. Once he played a song, her pulse seemed to relax until the next listener called in and couldn't wait for their next date. One even tried to figure out which part of town they were going. She'd been curious herself, but thankfully Andrew only dropped one hint, that their date had to do with Christmas.

The doorbell rang, and she startled out of her thoughts. She looked at herself another final time in the mirror, took a deep, calming breath, and said a prayer for peace and clarity before opening the front door. Andrew stood there in a light gray polo, layered with a blue two-button jacket and denim jeans. The smile he gave her shifted her insides, and she felt herself wobble.

"Are you ready?" he asked.

"Let me grab my bag and keys." She went to the foyer table and collected her things before he whisked her out the door to his waiting car. She caught sight of a man in her bushes. "Thank you," she said, as Andrew slid into the driver's seat and shut the door. She looked out the tinted windows. "Believe it or not, I'd forgotten for a moment about the cameras."

"I did as well when you opened the door."

She hid her grin, hoping he meant what she thought he had. "Where are we off to?"

"There's a new Mexican restaurant I've been meaning to try. I hear the food is great, and it has a patio that overlooks a large pond."

"It does sound nice."

"And practical. The cameras can be at a distance, allowing us to enjoy our meal. I hope you don't mind, I mentioned to Michael you weren't a fan of cameras. It was the only way to hopefully pull him back some."

"How did he take the news about Monday?"

"He wants us to reschedule to another day next week."

"I wish I had my calendar, but I'm pretty sure I have nothing going on Thursday. Will that work for you?"

"I'm free after the show. I've already dragged you to a food truck and made the plans for tonight, you pick what we do."

"You didn't drag me. I was willing. It's not every day I eat corn dogs from a food truck."

"Your first?"

"Second, but I enjoyed it more this time." Shoot. She sounded like she was flirting, but she meant it. "Last time I was digging in the garden when someone brought the volunteers lunch. I was so covered in dirt, even my corn dog tasted sandy."

"Maybe Michael was right," she caught him mumbling. "Next time we'll go somewhere nicer." He turned into a Mexican restaurant and parked.

"Whatever Michael said, don't listen to him. I've eaten at food trucks plenty of times, and it was perfect for our impromptu meeting. Besides, ice cream and corn dogs are two of my favorite things."

"Ice cream?" He raised an eyebrow. "And how did I not know this?"

"What can I say, I'm full of surprises. Now, are you going to jog around the car to let me out, or are we going to keep the cameras waiting?" Heaven help her. She didn't know what she was saying anymore. Her words were coming out faster than her head could keep up.

His grin drew her own. "Maybe we'll keep them waiting." He turned the car off, but his eyes never strayed from hers.

She was staring in surprise, and as shocking as his words were at first, Julia Nicole Morgan didn't care. She wanted to be there with him. She wanted to forget the entire bargain they'd made and be on a real date, as they enjoyed so long ago.

"Julia," he whispered, his hazel eyes growing soft. There was a slight blue tint within them she had never noticed before. Was it from the way the sun filtered through the windows? She wasn't sure but she wanted to lean in and see for herself. She watched as his eyes seem to ask permission for something she didn't understand, but when his gaze trailed to her lips, she knew, and her heart was ready.

He pulled back suddenly. "Maybe you were right. We can't keep Michael waiting." Andrew cleared his throat as he got out of the car, but it was the beat of her heart that jogged in sequence with Andrew as he came around to the passenger side door and opened it. "Lady Julia."

Goodness, her emotions were all over the place, and she didn't know how to tether them. She needed a minute, or ten, to pull herself together, but she was good at playacting— her niece was a great instructor. "Thank you, kind sir," she said as he assisted her out and closed the door behind her.

They walked into the restaurant, and it seemed all the commotion stopped. Then the flash of cameras began, and even those who'd been eating before pulled out phones and took pictures. Two servers approached. "Your table is ready. If you'll follow us."

As they were led to an outdoor patio that was strangely empty, she leaned close to Andrew. "Does everyone know who we are and why we're here?"

Andrew shrugged as the server placed menus on the table and motioned for them to sit. "Jan will be your server. She'll be here momentarily."

"Thank you," she and Andrew said in unison, taking opposite sides of the table. Julia waited until they were alone and looked around, taking in the beauty of the large pond and the colorful hardwoods, some of which were dropping their leaves. "Seems rather strange to be the only ones during a midday lunch rush. It's beautiful though."

"I'm sure Michael took special care that there wouldn't be any interruptions for this date."

"I see." She lifted a menu from the table and handed it to him.

He flipped it open and began scanning. "Back to Thursday's date. Since you have a thing for corn dogs and ice cream, too bad there's none on the menu."

"I think for this occasion, a chimichanga will do. But for Thursday, let's have ice cream. By the time you're off the air, I will have already eaten and be interested in dessert. Will that work for you? There is an ice cream shop that I love in the next county. It's not far."

"The county you wanted for your next garden?"

"Same. I try to shop locally as much as I can, either here or there. Besides, they have the best ice cream you'll ever taste."

"Then we'll go. While we're there, will you show me the property you were looking at?"

"You'd want to see it?"

"Why wouldn't I? I'm interested—"

"Welcome to Las Abuelas. My name is Jan, and I'll be serving you. What would you care to drink?"

"Sweet tea for me," Julia said, before turning from the server to admire the lovely view. That's when she noticed a man several yards away, holding a camera.

"Did you want to order now or wait until I come back with the drinks?"

Julia looked to Andrew to see his response, but he was waiting for her to answer. "I think we're ready." After they'd placed their orders, Julia leaned back in her chair and searched the scenery for more cameras. "Do you remember the kids' books and games, *Where's Waldo*? I'm playing a similar game called Where are the Cameras? I found one. Want to help me find the others?"

"Do you really want to know where they are? Or is it better just to know they're there?"

"I'm not sure." Her gaze kept searching. She had to think of a way to ease this worry beginning to overtake her. *Why is this so difficult for me when it's easy for others? I'm not a fearful person. Well, normally. No, I don't like heights or flying, or cameras. I love helping people, serving, making a difference, and through those acts, the Lord has given me opportunities to tell others about Him. Yes, I love people, but I don't like large settings of people because it's overwhelming, but small group settings, or one on one, I'm in my element.* Another thought came to her. She knew what to do.

"Juls, are you all right?"

The use of her nickname pulled her gaze back to him. "I will be." But her stomach still churned into knots, and knowing the cameras were pointing at them, it was as if the lenses gave off rays that burned into her skin. To distract herself from the feeling, she asked, "Have you heard anything else about Michael's plans for our last date?"

"Not yet, and it means he's going all out."

"Is that a good or bad thing?"

"Depends on how you look at it. Hopefully, it will be a night we can enjoy together."

Julia hoped so as well, because if nothing came of her feelings for Andrew by the end of these weeks, she wanted a different ending than him disappearing into the night.

There had never been another woman who made Andrew

feel alive and want to be a better man. She lit up his world with her smile, kindness, and the love she seemed to radiate to everyone. So, when she mentioned at the end of dinner that she wanted to meet the camera crew, he was taken aback at the timing, but not surprised. She took them desserts—that she paid for herself, even though it should have been Michael's dime—and they stood around talking for nearly thirty minutes. Julia had found out more about them and their families in that time than he had in the years he'd been working at the station. She even asked if she could pray with them before they left.

She explained later, on the drive to her home, that her motive had been to help her battle her fear of cameras by getting to know the people behind them. She continued to share that while she was talking with them, she realized she was there to show them the love of Christ and pray with them. She made it clear that fear wasn't from God, but that since she was fifteen, her fears had brought her closer to Him in faith. She prayed and rested more in His word, and she hadn't had a panic attack in years, but fear still lingered.

But Andrew noticed that fear hadn't stopped her from living or putting herself out there.

He thought of it that night as he lay in bed. If only he could be so open about his faith. It wasn't something you did at the radio station, but maybe he could get to know people in the way that Julia had tonight.

He reminded himself that he was a work in progress, slowly becoming more like Jesus, and when he thought of Julia, he saw them doing that together. An image of them, married, reading the Bible together, filled his thoughts, and joy washed over him. Iron sharpens iron.

Where was that verse?

He grabbed his phone and Bible off the nightstand and texted Julia.

Do you know where in scripture it talks about iron sharping iron?

Proverbs, I think. Let me look it up.

Of course, he could look it up for himself, but texting Julia was a better option.

She responded a moment later. *Proverbs 27:17. Doing some studying?*

Before I head to bed.

I'm about there.

I had a great time tonight.

I did too. We should do it again on Thursday. She sent a smiley face.

LOL! I won't miss it. Have a good night's sleep.

You do the same.

Thursday. That meant he had to wait almost a full week before seeing her again. Could he wait that long?

Eleven

Within minutes, Andrew would take the elevator to the parking garage and meet Julia where he'd asked her to park. She stared in the direction Andrew would come from, and her heart lit with anticipation. He'd signed off the airways, sending his listeners into a song, and Julia smiled as she lowered the volume of the car radio. She'd missed him this past week. The days seemed longer, and last night as she tried to fall asleep, she admitted to herself that his texts weren't enough. But could she tell him?

Julia took a long, calming breath, and a sigh escaped her lips. Maybe that was the problem between them years ago. She was the reason he never returned. She'd never had the strength to tell him how she truly felt. She had tried once, but the words wouldn't come. He had said he understood, but had he doubted once he was away?

No. He knew, even if she hadn't spoken the words. He had looked her in the eye and made promises. So many promises that her tender heart soared, and she believed every word.

That was the problem, even now her heart and mind were conflicted with the past and how she still felt for him. She wanted to trust him, to believe him, yet she still held herself back. Could she take that leap of faith?

A knock at the window startled her, and her gaze flew up to find Andrew peering into the car. His lazy smile lightened the nagging concerns she had. Apprehension wasn't a bad thing; it meant she'd learned from her mistakes, but how many more would she make where Andrew was concerned?

She unlocked the door, and he slid into the passenger seat. "You looked deep in thought."

"You scared me." She started the engine, avoiding his question, then backed out of the parking space.

"I see that, but still, is everything all right?"

How could she answer? She could sense his eyes were on her, waiting, but she didn't want to have this conversation while she was driving, but it was the open door she'd been waiting for to tell him how she felt. "Andrew, I—"

"I've missed you, Julia," he said, softly. "I know this isn't part of our agreement, but I'd like to see you more than on Mondays and Fridays."

"You would?"

"I would, if you'll allow me?"

Relief washed over her. He was going down the same path she wanted to tread. "I'd like that."

"Can I call you?"

She chuckled. "You could've called me before now."

"I almost called several times this week just to hear your voice."

This was it, the pivotal moment that she wanted, and she didn't want to go through it less than completely honest, no matter what happened. "Then, I think I should admit something: I wish you had. I've missed you too."

Andrew cleared his throat and looked out the window, but she caught his smile in the reflection. Perhaps it matched her own. "Thank you for picking me up from Birmingham. I know it was out of the way."

"I don't mind. I like to drive." She shrugged. "It relaxes me."

"Oh, I caught Michael on the way out of the office. He said he was going to be in our neck of the woods and asked if

I wanted to catch a ride back with him. I told him that would be great."

"I'm sure he'd be close. With cameras and all. What did he say when you told him we were going for ice cream?"

"To have fun. He seems more laid back lately. I don't know what the difference has been, but believe me, I don't mind. So enough about Michael, where are you taking me first, to the garden or for the best ice cream in town?"

Twenty minutes later, Julia pulled up to a rundown area on the outskirts of downtown Fletcher County. As she put her car in park, she still couldn't understand why the city turned her down. It was two blocks with weeds, a rusted basketball goal, desecrated buildings, and a chain link fence encircling the entire area, reminding her of a juvenal rehabilitation center.

"Why would the city block your proposal? This place looks condemned."

She glanced at him in amazement that their thoughts were aligned once more. "I have no idea." She got out of the car, leaving her door open.

Andrew did the same and came to her. "Do you think it's the ground? Maybe it was a landfill at one time."

"I had someone check into it, and it came back clear. Several years ago, the city had soil testing done, and it also came back fine. The area was an old mining town. I found a few pictures, and they had a garden here. I'd like to bring it back."

"I know you will."

"I wish I had your faith."

He turned to her. "You don't give yourself enough credit."

"I'd like to say you're right, but it's the opposite. I give myself plenty of credit. It's the Lord who takes me down a notch or two. He blessed me with a wonderful mind for business, and there's not a blink of fear or hesitation. It's like I knew which way to go in the dealings with my company. There was a certainty that I can't explain, but this . . ." She held out her arms. "I'm at a loss. This is what He's called me to do, and my steps are so unsure. How is that even possible when all of this is for His glory?" Her hands fell to her sides. "Maybe I misunderstood. Maybe this is all a mistake."

"Juls." Andrew lifted her chin with his finger, and her heart skipped a beat. "I believe it's always good to ask the Lord if He'll reveal the motives of our hearts when serving Him. Like, 'Lord, is it for your glory or for mine?' But in the weeks since we've reconnected, it's obvious that what you're doing isn't a mistake. I think you understood the Lord's calling to help others perfectly, because from what I've seen, you are being the hands and feet of Christ. You're even helping widows." He took a step closer and cupped her jaw within his palm.

Her eyes closed at his touch. "Andrew," her voice whispered between them before her gaze fluttered to his.

"You radiate Christ, and I'm drawn to you. Don't you see, you're an amazing woman, Juls. I hope it doesn't come as a surprise, but I want more of this with you. I'd like to see you after all this is over, if you'll have me."

Hope. She'd tried to stomp it out at the beginning of their bargain, but here he was, smiling that soft smile of his, urging her to agree. "Are you sure?"

"More than anything."

Julia opened her mouth to answer when his phone rang. Andrew continued to look deep into her eyes and made no move to answer the call. "Shouldn't you get that?"

Andrew's gaze slid to her lips, and for a moment, she was sure he was going to kiss her, but instead, he dropped his hand and took a step back. He reached in his pocket and answered. "Michael."

Julia watched as Andrew's gaze narrowed at the ground,

then intensified as he spun and looked off into the distance. He started walking back to the car and got in. She wasn't sure what was being said, but whatever it was, Michael's call wasn't a good one.

She headed to the car, slid into the driver's seat, and fastened her seat belt. All Andrew did as she drove to the ice cream shop was grunt a couple of times in what seemed like agreement to whatever Michael was saying, then, abruptly, he hung up. He looked out the window, and his frown was plain to see. "Everything all right?" She tried to keep a neutral expression, but surely he heard the concern in her voice.

"I don't know yet."

"Do we need to cancel our ice cream?"

"No, Michael is waiting for us there. If I'd known—"

"Known what?"

"Forget I said anything."

That was easier said than done, because once they arrived at the ice cream shop, Andrew was just as cool as the temperature in the building. He barely spoke, rarely smiled, and when he did, it was forced. Whatever had happened between him and Michael during that call, Julia knew it wasn't good news.

She hoped it had nothing to do with her, but now as she drove to her sister's for dinner, something within her sensed she was the link to it all.

As Julia rang the doorbell, she took a fortifying breath and straightened her shoulders to try to hide the distress she was feeling. "I got it!" she heard Stacey yelling from the other side of the door. The door swung open, and there stood Princess Stacey in all of her pink glory and sparkling plastic crown.

"Princess Stacey." She curtsied.

"Rise, my faithful companion. I demand a hug right this instant. Mother has been a villain all day."

She lifted Stacey in her arms and gave her a big squeeze, sending giggles into the air. "A villain?" she murmured. "Don't let her hear you say that, or it would be to the dungeon you'd go."

"Gallows, you mean."

"That bad, huh? What did you do?"

"I took Mr. Astronaut again from Bobby's room to play tea party. I spilled fruit punch all over my room and on him. When I saw Mommy was doing a load of clothes, I threw him in to be cleaned. It didn't work." She tilted her head to the side. "Did you know fruit punch can turn white sheets pink?"

"I never really thought about it before, but I guess it can."

"It turned the towels pink too, even the ones I used to clean up."

"I see." And she did. Her niece was high energy and into everything. "What happened to Mr. Astronaut?"

"His stuffing came out from his head. Bobby started crying, but I told him all he had to do was put a hat on him. I have some hats." She pointed to her head, though she wasn't wearing one. "He told me to leave Mr. Astronaut alone."

"Well, now that I'm here, maybe I can help with Mr. Astronaut. Tell Bobby to bring him to me. I'll see what I can do." She set her niece on her feet and watched as she ran toward Bobby's room. Julia found her sister in the kitchen cooking.

"Finally," she said, draining the grease from the hamburger meat. "I need your help. I know I can do it later, but it would be too late. Mr. Astronaut is in need of surgery, stat."

"I'm already on it."

"Thank you." She dumped the meat into the pot of spaghetti sauce and angel hair pasta. She began to stir.

"Bobby has been upset for hours. I don't know why Stacey keeps taking the toy."

"Have you asked her?" Julia went to the cabinet and took out a stack of plates.

"No, but I probably should. So how was your date with Andrew?"

"It was different. People recognized us and as we were leaving, came up for selfies and autographs." What else could she say that wouldn't raise her sister's ire? Julia was about to dive into a pool of unknowns, and she wasn't sure where the life preserver was located. "Since dinner is almost ready, let's wait until later so we don't get interrupted."

Her sister nodded, looking around. "Good plan. I'll grab the spaghetti, garlic bread, and silverware. You get napkins and drinks. I'll call the kids." She left for the dining room with the pot of spaghetti.

"Auntie, Auntie! You're on TV! Are you in love with Sir Andrew?" Stacey yelled from the living room.

It took a second before her brain caught on to what her niece was saying. She rushed into the living room, and her heart skid to a stop. Her face grew hot as she watched Andrew cup her jaw in his palm. She remembered the moment and how he made her feel cared for, wanted, but now, she felt tears prick her eyes at the scene unfolding of her and Andrew about to kiss. She hadn't realized she was leaning into him when his cell rang.

Kaylie grabbed the remote and turned off the television. When Julia met her sister's worried gaze, unbridled pain drove itself into her heart, deep, right to her very soul.

Twelve

It was nearly one in the morning, and Andrew sat on Julia's doorstep, waiting for her to arrive home. He'd hoped she hadn't learned that their intimate time together in Fletcher County had been watched by millions of people across the country, but given her unreturned calls, she had.

He didn't know what to do about his job, his future, and especially how he'd convince Julia he had known nothing about Michael's plan. It all made sense now—Michael's questions, wanting to know the time and the place where they'd be, and why they'd be visiting Fletcher County. He'd even used Julia's fear of cameras against her, hiding them out of sight.

On the way back to Birmingham, Michael had tried to justify his actions and convince him that he'd had every right, given their agreement, but he admitted he had no idea the connection between them ran so deep. It was the reason for his call, to stop the kiss before it was too late. And for that one act, Andrew was grateful. He had never truly kissed Julia, no matter how much he had wanted to, or how she'd seemed to need the assurance in high school, he'd always held off. It was an ache, a need he'd never had with another woman, a desire that held him in check over the years. He knew the Lord had placed her in his life because the strength of his love hadn't dimmed with the passing of time. He never questioned that love. The question had always been, was he worthy of her and would they ever find their way back to each other? He knew the answers now, but where Julia lacked faith, he had enough for them both. With the Lord, nothing is impossible.

A car in the distance slowed, and as it neared, he could tell it was Julia's. He didn't rise from the steps of her home until she turned the car off and got out. The security light came on, and she avoided eye contact as she neared. He wanted to go to her but held himself in place and prayed again for his words to ring true to her ears.

"Juls?"

"Don't call me that." She walked past him to the front door.

"Can we talk?"

She fumbled with her keys as she tried to open the door. "We have nothing to talk about."

"Please. You need to let me explain."

She kept her back to him and changed to the next key. "You don't need to explain. I think I finally see clearly."

"No. I don't think you do. I had nothing to do with this. I was just as surprised as you. It was Michael."

She spun and faced him. Her eyes were red, as if she'd been crying for a while. "Really? Not as surprised as me to find Stacey watching us in a private moment, or when she asked if I was in love with Sir Andrew. I felt my heart break in two, knowing that the man I love not only broke my heart once, but that I was foolish enough to allow him to crush it a second time?"

Her words cut through him. His own heart stumbled out a frantic beat. "You love me." On instinct, he reached out, but she spun back to the door, avoiding his touch.

"And sometimes love isn't meant to be."

"I love you too, Julia. I've never stopped."

"Then you have a terrible way of showing it." The door opened, and she walked inside. He quickly followed her, but she turned to him, stopping him in the doorway. "I don't want you here, Drew."

"Juls, please. It's Andrew."

"No. Andrew was someone who disappeared one night. He told me he loved me, and he'd be back, but he never returned."

"If you let me explain."

"I waited up night after night for him. Weeks. Months went by, and not a word. I prayed for his safety. I cried myself to sleep. I was so worried something terrible had happened to him. But something had, over time, and he became a painful memory. And that is where he needs to stay."

Speechless, Andrew stood there and watched as the door closed, and the security light flicked off. He dropped to the steps and palmed his face. How could he fix this? He didn't know, but he wouldn't give up trying.

Picking himself back up, he headed to Michael's. They needed to talk, and it couldn't wait until morning.

Andrew stood at Julia's sister's front door, but he had yet to ring the doorbell. He wasn't sure what he was going to say. With Julia ignoring him and Michael threatening his job because Julia canceled their Friday date, his back was against the wall. Regardless of how hard his boss pushed for Julia and him to fix this, his visit with Kaylie was a plea for help, not for the show, but because he couldn't imagine living his life without Julia in it. He needed an ally, and who better than her own sister. Now only if he could get her to agree.

The door yanked open, startling him. Kaylie stood on the

other side of the door with a hand on her hip and a smirk on her lips. "Plan to stand out here all day? Or are you trying to huff and puff my door down? My door cam is catching the exact sounds."

He smiled at her comment. "It doesn't seem to be working."

"No, but after the first ten minutes, I would have given up and knocked."

"I don't give up so easily."

"If you plan on having a future with my sister, then that way of thinking will serve you well." She opened the door fully. "Might as well come in."

"Thank you." He stepped over the threshold and glanced into the living room, waiting for her to lead the way. She motioned to the sectional. "Have a seat, this might take a while. I have a lot of questions for you."

"I'd be happy to answer them, as long as you hear me out." He sat, more nervous than he was to begin with. Maybe this was a bad idea. Kaylie sat in the recliner across from him. "Where would you like for me to begin?"

"What brings you by, exactly?"

"I need your help winning your sister back."

"I thought that might be the case, but who said you had her affection?"

"I know your sister cares for me deeply. That's what makes this situation so difficult. I had nothing to do with Michael's plan to televise our private moments together. And I promise you, I had no knowledge of what he was up to, or I would never have allowed it to happen in the first place. I could never think of hurting her."

"So, this isn't a farce, your affection for Julia? To do whatever you can or whatever it takes to get your dream job?"

"No. Never. I love your sister, and that's why I'm here. It has nothing to do with a job or what Michael wants."

"What does he want from you?"

"For me to fix this, but this visit is for me. I'd rather lose the job than lose Julia again. I understand why she still feels pain and hurt from my past actions. I still haven't come to terms with what happened or stopped regretting that day. If I had to do it over again, I would. Done something differently, tried harder, anything. I can't let her go this time."

Stacey swept into the room and ran to him. "Sir Andrew! I didn't know you were coming." She reached for his neck and hugged him. "Would you like to have some tea?"

Kaylie cleared her throat. "Sweetie, Andrew and I are talking. It's rude to interrupt."

"But tea?"

"You need to go back and finish cleaning your room."

"But it's done."

Kaylie gave her a frown and slid to the edge of the recliner. "You don't want me to check. If I do, and there's a mess, no tea party for a week, and you'll have to hang up your slippers."

"I think I should double-check just in case." She ran toward the hallway. Giving him a backward glance, she waved. He gave a light chuckle and turned back to Kaylie, who was shaking her head.

"Don't encourage her. She's a lot like me at that age, but don't tell her I said so. She'll never let me live it down." She smiled. "Now, where were we? Oh, yes, your high school relationship with my sister has been a mystery all these years, and I'm more than ready to hear about it."

"Julia never told you?"

"What happened between you? Not a word. It's the only part of her life she has totally shut me out of. And I have to tell you, Drew, if you want my help, I need to know before making my decision."

"It was graduation." He felt himself drifting back to

another place and time, to how the rain threatened heavy in the air. While things over the years had grown hazy, he'd never forget standing on the high school football field waiting for Julia's name to be called. He continually sought her gaze from across the rows of students, but when her brown eyes finally caught his . . . "When your sister smiled at me before she received her diploma, I knew that night I was going to propose to her."

"Wait. What? You proposed?"

"I did. Later that night."

Kaylie's shoulders slumped, and she looked toward a collection of pictures on the mantle. He assumed she stared at the wood-framed portrait of her and Julia hugging with bright smiles on their faces, as if they shared a joke. "I don't get it." She stood and strolled to the window. "Granted, I was in Italy, but she barely mentioned you, except that you were popular and cute." She turned to look at him. "You had a class project together."

"We did. It was the first time we had talked since she moved back. Honestly, she had this strange effect on me. She made me nervous, and I'd forget what I was saying around her. That project started it all for us."

"Wow." She shook her head, obviously taking in all he was sharing, but he could also see the questions fluttering across her face. "How long had you been seeing each other?"

"A little over a year."

"That long. I had no idea. Did my parents know?"

He glanced away. "Yes. It wasn't a secret how we felt for each other. We were happy."

"If you were so happy, why did you walk away from her? A proposal and break-up, in a span of an hour or two, doesn't make sense."

He glanced to his hands. "The morning of graduation, I learned I was accepted for an internship at a radio station in

Seattle. She knew I was excited about the opportunity and what it meant to me if I was accepted. I hadn't had the time to tell Julia I was leaving, so that night, I took her to the pond you had at the back of your house. I shared the news with her, and she wasn't as thrilled as I had expected. I explained this was great for our future because if she'd have me, I couldn't wait to be her husband. I got down on my knee and proposed. She said yes before I could even finish asking." He smiled at the memory, but a numbing awareness of what was yet to come followed. "That night we made plans for our future just as the rains came and drenched us from head to toe. We ran into the house, where we met your father in the foyer putting on his raincoat and about to look for us. Julia immediately showed him the ring, but the excitement for the occasion wasn't shared. At first, I thought it was because I hadn't asked his permission, which I planned to do that evening, but I was so carried away by the day and my unexpected internship I couldn't wait. But when I left, your father followed me out."

"What did he say?"

"That I wasn't good enough for his daughter, and coming from a broken home, I wouldn't know what the word commitment meant, since it wasn't shown in my home. Not only that, but that my career path would lead us to the poor house. It was as if he knew my fears. Each word he spoke dug deep. Yes, I was afraid to let someone into my life because loving someone and then watching them leave tears the heart out. The aftermath, the financial struggles . . . I saw my mom go through it trying to raise me and my brother alone. I took odd jobs when I was younger to put food on the table, then joined a school program that allowed me to leave during school to work. Yes, I was afraid of commitment, but that was until I fell in love with Julia."

"Drew?" Kaylie leaned forward and touched his hand.

"He made me believe I would never be enough for her." Andrew's throat clogged with emotion, and when he spoke, he could barely whisper. "I was a nineteen-year-old boy with dreams of a girl, a girl I'd been in love with since your mom tugged her into the preschool room and our eyes met. Eyes that have haunted me over the years. If you must know the truth, it wasn't this job that prompted me to search Julia out, I'd always known where she was. It was the Lord leading me to go to her. He used the job as an opening to see her again."

"What are you going to do?"

"I love your sister, Kaylie, and I'm not giving up this time. I need your help convincing her to let me back in."

"I thought you'd never ask."

Thirteen

With dread in her chest, Julia stumbled to her sister's front door holding two food carriers in each hand. Her purse dangled from her right wrist and a key ring from the other. It wasn't the bulk of the casseroles or the oddity of them as she made her way up the stone steps to the house that caused her alarm, but knowing who would be joining them for Thanksgiving dinner.

Why would her sister invite Andrew?

She just couldn't fathom it, especially knowing how he'd used her for his personal gain, and let everyone be a witness to her humiliation.

Julia tapped the toe of her boot against the bottom of the door, and within moments, the door swung open to reveal the man himself holding her niece's hand.

"Lady Julia." Stacey released Andrew's hand and curtsied. "Sir Andrew and I have been waiting for your arrival."

"We have," Andrew finally spoke, and her heart squeezed at the timber of his voice, the voice she'd missed after leaving a message on his phone that she was done with the games they were playing and would take her chances with the city however they decided.

"Can I help take something to the kitchen?" He reached for her burdens, but she drew back.

"If you'll let me in, I can take them to the kitchen."

"Oh, of course." He stepped aside, and she hurried past.

Sounds of a football game could be heard in the background as she made her way to the kitchen.

Julia set her load on the kitchen counter. "You made pies?"

"Andrew made them. Pumkin." Kaylie slid the two pies into the oven. "And don't look at me like that, all frowny. Today is a day to be thankful."

"I'm finding myself a little lacking in the thankful department, with you-know-who here."

Kaylie drew near and leaned her head against Julia's. "There's more to the story. Give him a chance to explain." She met her gaze and smiled. "Promise me you'll at least hear him out?"

"What did he say? This isn't like you. You know how hurt I am by what he did. It's like you don't care. You invited him to *Thanksgiving,* of all holidays."

"Just promise me, Juls, then decide your next steps." She looked around at the food-ladened counters and clapped her hands. "Another hour and we'll be ready. I'll give Dean a heads up, so it won't be a shock when he has to DVR the game."

"I'm glad Dean made it for Thanksgiving this year."

"Me too. Bringing another partner on with his hunting guide service has had many advantages. He's booked up for the season, but he's home today and for the rest of the weekend, so I can't complain."

Kaylie left her standing in the middle of the kitchen, replaying her words about Andrew. She'd asked her to promise to allow him to explain his actions, but she couldn't bring herself to do it."

"Juls," Andrew said as he entered the kitchen. "Do you think we can talk? Kaylie mentioned we have an hour before dinner is ready." His hazel eyes pleaded.

She wanted to say "no" flat out, but she found it difficult

to refuse the man standing in front of her. His worried expression marred his features, and she felt herself nod a silent agreement before her head registered what she'd done.

This was the most important moment in Andrew's life, but only incoherent words and half apologies bounced around his mind, making a muddled mess. What was he supposed to do, lay everything at her feet and hope she understood his heart?

She pointed to the gazebo where they had tea with Stacey some weeks ago. "Will this work?"

"Perfectly." At least he could speak. When they reached the gazebo, he pulled out a chair for her, but she remained standing, arms crossed.

"I'm not sure how you got my sister on your side, but it must have been a good story. She's hard to persuade."

"I told her the truth. I promise you, Julia, I had no idea what Michael was up to, but if I had known . . . it was meant to be a private moment. After everything I've done to protect you from Michael's schemes and cameras . . . do you honestly believe I would deliberately hurt you?"

Her arms slid to her sides. "Yes. You deliberately hurt me once before. Why not a second time?"

His heart was breaking at the moisture pooling in her eyes. He had to make this right and somehow correct the past. "I've never meant to hurt you. Ever."

"But you did. I'm afraid to trust what you're saying. You said you loved me once before, and you couldn't wait for us to start our lives together, then you disappeared."

"Will you let me explain?"

She held up a hand. "Then years later, you walk back into my life for a dream job you've always wanted, and somehow, I'm the only one who can give you your promotion, if we date on TV. Then you tell me you care about me. You want to spend more time together, but within hours, we're on TV about to kiss. All the while, the station is capturing the highest ratings they've ever received. Do you not see how this looks? Can you not understand how I feel? Like I've been used." A tear ran down her cheek, and she quickly wiped it away.

Her words hit him hard, and he pulled out one of the patio chairs and almost fell into it. "It seems you've already made up your mind." He looked to his hand clenched in his lap. "I'm sorry, Julia. I'm sorry for getting you involved in all this."

"I re-played what happened at Fletcher County and the rest of our time together that day. I could tell something was wrong. After you received that call." A moment ticked by before she sat in the chair he had pulled out earlier for her.

"I promise you, I didn't know what had happened until Michael called. He told me where the cameras were hidden, and I became furious. I didn't tell you then because I thought if I had a chance to speak with Michael, I could get him to change his mind. Obviously, it didn't work. He continually reminded me of our agreement and his right to do as he saw fit."

"You should have told me when we got back in the car, after he hung up."

"I should have, but I thought I could make it go away." Was she softening toward him? He met her eyes, and his gaze lingered there, watching, waiting for a sign of what to do or say next.

"I'm sorry that things worked out as they did. I hope

Michael still gives you another shot to host the morning show."

"It doesn't matter to me. The only reason I went along with Michael's idea was because I thought it was a way for us to reconnect and for me to be a part of your life again. How everything worked out, I thought the Lord was giving us another chance."

"You didn't want the job?"

"I did, I do, but it means little without you. I thought—"

"You thought what?"

He wasn't sure how to respond now that he knew her true thoughts, so he said nothing. More time ticked by, and the expectant look on her face slipped, as did her gaze. She took out a tissue from her pants pocket and dotted her eyes. He needed time to think. She believed him about Michael, but there was still their past to deal with and her trust in him.

"How did Michael handle the news when I called off our date last Friday?"

"As you can imagine, not so well. A threat here, a threat there. Then after a day or two of ignoring me, he went on with business like normal. It was odd. But then, in the place of our date, he ran some extra footage he'd taken in the garden. He shared how many people you'd been serving since you'd been on the show. He'd obviously been filming you out in public, which I'm starting to realize is his MO. There was also a video of you taking seniors to doctors' appointments. He praised the work that you'd been doing in the community, though."

Her mouth opened slightly. "Really? I had no idea. I'm not sure if I should be upset or thank him for . . ."

"For?"

She met his gaze, and her brown eyes searched his.

"Doing what you did from the very first day. Telling people about the garden." She looked away and stared into the distance, and he said nothing more.

Fourteen

"Sir Andrew? Lady Julia?" Stacey's sweet voice broke through the quiet between her and Andrew. Finding them sitting several feet apart, she gathered their hands one by one and led them toward the house. "Thanksgiving dinner is ready."

Julia meant it to be a quick glance at the man by her side, but the prayer she'd offered to the Lord a moment ago seemed to come back answered in a blink of an eye, and she struggled to look away. Andrew was telling her the truth about Michael, and he'd done everything to protect her as he suggested. She'd seen it with her own eyes, then why did this reluctance to trust him not go away? Yet, she knew the answer. No matter how things were now, the past still haunted her for answers.

They entered the dining room, and Julia introduced Andrew to the family that had arrived while they'd been outside. Several family members brought guests, and before she knew it, extra chairs were pulled out as everyone gathered around the table. She and Andrew sat next to one another, their chairs snug together to accommodate everyone at the table.

Dean cleared his throat and stood. "I want to thank you all for joining Kaylie and me for Thanksgiving this year. Before we start, I'd like for us to go around the table and share what we're thankful for this year. And to start off, I believe I'll go first. I'm thankful for the bounty of food on this table and to those who prepared it."

Kaylie looked at her husband with laughing eyes. "I'm thankful for my husband, who catches me off guard at times and reminds me he does have a serious bone in his body. I'm also thankful to the Lord for blessing us with family and new friends." She looked in Andrew's direction, and affection shone in her eyes as she smiled at him.

How is this possible? Julia blinked in confusion as the next person began to share. She sat back in her chair and leaned into Andrew's shoulder, noticing the clean, fresh scent he wore wherever he went. It was hard enough being this close to him when her heart was waging a battle between forgiveness and fear. She didn't need the extra temptation to move closer. Instead, she tucked her hands in her lap to give herself boundaries before she did something she'd regret. "My sister," she whispered, "what else did you tell her besides what happened with Michael?"

Andrew turned his face slightly in her direction, causing them to be only inches apart. He looked at her then with such deep longing. "Everything."

Her chest squeezed at the meaning. Was he suggesting *everything* from their past? She couldn't wait another minute to find out. "Meet me in the living room." Julia quietly rose from her chair and almost tip-toed out of the dining room, where seconds later, Andrew joined her. She looked back over her shoulder to make sure they were alone. "What do you mean by *everything*?"

"Our past. Graduation—"

Julia shook her head in disbelief. "Why? What good would it do for her to know? This was between us."

"Yes, but with what happened with Michael, and you shutting me out of your life, I needed advice and direction. I said this to you before, and I'll keep saying it until you believe me: I love you. And despite all my past mistakes, you still love me too. How can I not want to work things out between us?"

What he said was true. She was trying to shut him out, but the door to her heart wouldn't close. The Lord made sure of that, reminding her of scriptures of forgiveness, that no matter how badly Andrew had hurt her, she needed to trust the Lord and follow His leading. And right now, He was telling her to listen. But she had one question to ask, one question that had changed her seventeen-year-old heart the Lord was still mending. The same question that continued to burn her soul all these years later. "Why did you leave?"

Andrew ran his hand down his jawline. Anguish filled his hazel eyes as he looked at her, pleading, before he spoke a word. She noticed again he wasn't the young man he once was. Though still so very handsome, there were new lines between his brows. They appeared when he was in deep thought, as he was now. There were differences, and they reminded her of how much time they'd missed from each other's lives. Time they'd never get back. *And how much time I've been in love with you.* She became impatient at his silence. "Nothing to say?"

"I was afraid, Juls. I didn't grow up in a family like yours. I had no idea how to be a husband when I never saw one growing up. I was afraid of making you unhappy. I had no job prospects, only direction. How was I going to support us?"

"We would have figured it out."

"Perhaps, but how long before you started being disappointed in me? Sorry we married? All I wanted was for you to be happy. Not fail you."

"But Andrew, you did, when you walked away."

He gave a slight nod as moisture filled his eyes. He glanced toward the door. "I know." His voice was husky. "If I could take it all back, I would."

"Leaving me?"

He bit his lip and shifted his weight. "Yes. I'd do things differently. It's why I spoke with Kaylie. I want another chance, Juls. I want what should have been."

Julia swallowed against the tears gathering at her throat. *Lord? What do I do?* There was no answer, only the pounding of her heart and an unbearable silence between them. "I believe you," she finally said. "All of it. Fletcher County. Michael. Why you left after graduation."

"I see fear in your eyes. And yet, you still love me."

He was right. She couldn't deny it. "I want to tell you that I want us to try again. That I want you to hold me and never let me go . . ."

"But you can't."

"No. I need time. To think. To pray. Will you give me time?"

"All that you need." He closed the distance between them and lifted her chin with his finger. "I will wait for you as long as you waited for me, and my entire life if need be." He placed a gentle kiss on her cheek before releasing her. "Please give Dean and Kaylie my apologies. I should go."

Stunned at his gentleness and how quickly she desired to run after him, all she could do was watch him stroll out of the house.

"Go after him!"

Julia jerked in surprise at her sister's voice and spun to see her standing in the hallway pointing at the door. "How long have you been listening?"

"Too long. What are you doing letting that man leave?"

"Since you heard, I need time, and he's willing to give it to me."

"It was Dad who made him stop seeing you, Juls."

"What?"

"The night of graduation, after he left, Dad told him he

wasn't good enough for you, that he'd amount to nothing, and you'd be unhappy."

"Andrew told you this?"

"Yes, everything. His proposing. How he meant every word he said that night. How Dad threatened to stop the marriage if he had to. Drew didn't even want to tell you what Dad had done because he's not here to defend himself. He didn't want to tarnish your image of our father. But we both know how persuasive Dad was and how nothing stopped him from getting what he wanted. If it hadn't been for him, you and Drew would have married. He never stopped loving you."

Julia flew through the room and swung the front door open. Andrew was getting into his car in the driveway. "Andrew! Wait!"

He looked up and caught her gaze.

"Hold on, Sis!" Kaylie grabbed her arm. "I gave permission for Michael to be out there."

She frowned. "Why?"

"To save Drew's job. Just be aware that whatever happens out there, it's for all to see."

Julia gave a quick nod and hurried out the door, meeting Andrew on the walkway. "First, I have to tell you that my sister gave Michael video access to the front of the house, so whatever happens out here is public."

"Then let's go inside." He started to lead the way, but she held fast to his arm, pulling them close. "Julia." He looked into her eyes. "The cameras."

"Is it true?" She shifted closer. "Was my father the reason you left?"

"Yes," he whispered.

"The thought of losing you again . . ." She couldn't bring herself to finish her sentence. Tears formed in her eyes.

He brushed a strand of hair from her face and continued

a path of tingles from her jawline to the nape of her hair. His lips were now closer and lingered above her mouth. "This isn't goodbye?"

"Only the beginning."

His lips grazed hers, and hers parted in response. He kissed her then, soft, sweet, inviting her to join in, but she was lost in the feel of him in her arms, the gentleness of his touch. She'd dreamt of this moment with this man for most of her life; she wouldn't rush it. She drew her arms around his neck and returned his kiss. Her fingers sought the back of his hairline, and as if giving permission, he deepened the kiss. It was as if their love was a symphony. It was the only way to describe the give and take, the way her heart soared, but also their need for each other, to never be separated again.

It wasn't until they heard a throat clearing that Julia startled within Andrew's arms. "Can we help you?" Andrew asked, keeping a loving arm around her.

The man held out two envelopes. "Delivery."

They accepted, thanked the man, and Julia was the first to open the card. She scanned the contents. "It's from Michael. We have our final date tomorrow night."

"But I don't understand. I made it clear that we were done." He scanned the invitation.

"I believe my sister might have something to do with this."

"We're to dine at 360 Grille."

"In Florence," she said, reading the address. "That's a little over two hours from here."

"I'll talk with Michael about this."

"No, let's do it." She smiled at him. "I think we deserve a night, don't you?"

"Are you sure?" His brows knitted together.

She nodded, giving him a quick peck on the lips. "I'm sure."

"Then we'll go."

"Good!" Kaylie said from the doorway. Dean had a hand around her hip, laughing. "Now, will you two get in here and join us for Thanksgiving?"

"Are you ready to join my family?" she asked, taking Andrew's arm. "My sister is a demanding one."

"More than ready."

Fifteen

Julia finished packing an overnight bag for her stay in Florence and set it by her front door. Her sister had said she didn't look very excited about her dinner with Andrew tonight, but her body was trying to recover from her lack of sleep as she'd lain awake thinking of him into the early morning hours, and regardless, her heart was doing some wild things within her chest. It started first thing this morning when a text from Andrew greeted her as her eyes had just begun to open. He, Michael, and the crew were heading out at dawn for their hotel, but he shared how much he missed her and how he couldn't wait until tonight.

"Are you about ready?" Kaylie asked, her hand firmly on her hip. "I keep finding you standing around the house, looking into outer space."

"What can I say, it seems my mind wants to stop and think of nothing but Andrew, and my feet agree, but my heart is pulsating like an erratic locator beacon, just waiting for him."

"Well, tell those feet and mind of yours to move because they're keeping you two apart."

Amused, Julia smiled. "Well, since you're driving, I'll have all the time I need to woolgather."

Kaylie's hand slipped to her side. "Mom used to say that all the time. Woolgathering," she said, giving Julia a tender look. "I miss her."

"I do too." She took the few steps between them and hugged her sister's neck, but before stepping away, said, "Who's woolgathering now?"

"Fine, it's not so bad on this side of things."

She chuckled, pulling her to arm's length. "You're a great big sister. Thank you for always being here for me and being my protector."

"With that independent streak of yours, with you running a multimillion dollar company and wanting to change the world, it's a hard job to look after you, but someone has to do it. It does have its perks though."

"Which is?"

Kaylie led her toward the living room. "I get to boss you around and tell you to hurry, or you won't be able to see Andrew before your date. We're late leaving as it is."

Julia's phone chimed from the coffee table, and she moved in that direction, giving her sister a teasing look. "I'll hurry," she said, but when she glanced at the call, she quickly answered. "Hello, this is Julia Morgan."

Andrew brushed a hand down his black sports jacket and made sure his white button-up shirt was tucked into his trousers. He was relieved he wasn't wearing a tie because with no sight of Julia, and the ring box in his right pocket, he was beginning to get warm and couldn't help fidgeting or pacing the hotel lobby near the elevators to the restaurant. She had called to say they'd be running late, but that was four hours ago, and when he called to see if she had arrived, he received no word. He ended up speaking with the check-in desk, and thankfully, she was in the hotel with her sister. He continued to catch Michael's disapproval though. Andrew tried to remind him that she wasn't technically late, not yet anyway, but that didn't seem to improve his mood.

Michael looked at his watch again and came to stand beside him. "She has three minutes."

He nodded. "I know."

And that was when Andrew saw her, coming down the hallway in a black pleated flare dress with a belt around her waist. It was when her gaze trained in on him that she smiled, and he knew he was done for. He wanted to whisk Julia away to kiss her soundly, then find a pastor somewhere to marry them, but he also knew Michael would stick to them like glue if they tried to get away. Too much had gone into this night and whatever Michael had planned, but there was no place he'd rather be than with her.

"Andrew," she said as she reached him. She leaned in, and he met her halfway, gently cupping her bare arm, then kissed her cheek. The tender look in her soft brown eyes as he pulled away warmed his soul.

He hadn't noticed where Michael had gone, but with the camera rolling and Julia at his side, it was time. "You ready to go up for dinner?"

"I am." The elevator doors opened a second later, and they both entered. They waited for the doors to close, and Julia was the first to speak. "I've missed you. I don't know what's going to happen tomorrow when this is all over, but—"

"The only thing that's going to happen, is tomorrow we won't be forced to display our relationship in front of cameras." He cupped her cheek and ran a thumb over the heart-shaped freckle on her jawline. "I've been dreaming of this moment."

"Of my freckle?"

It wasn't what he'd meant entirely, but the evening was

still young, and there was plenty of time to explain later. "Of course."

The elevator doors began to open, and they stepped back from each other and laughed, but Julia's laughter was short-lived as she noticed the view for the first time. Michael hadn't allowed Andrew in the restaurant earlier when the crew was setting up, and now Andrew was grateful to share the experience with her. "It's Wilson Lake."

"Drew and Julia, right this way please." A hostess escorted them to a table next to the window. "A server will be with you shortly."

Andrew pulled out Julia's chair before sitting. "Are you happy?"

"Very." She pointed to the line of trees along the waterway. "Can you imagine this view during the changing of the leaves? It's beautiful now, but I'm sure it would be magnificent from here."

"We can always come back."

"I'd like that."

A server approached and handed them menus. "Do you know what you'd like to drink?"

"Two sweet teas, please," Julia said, giving him a wink.

Andrew nodded his thanks and waited for their server to step away before meeting Julia's gaze. He was enjoying this relaxed side of her, but he couldn't stop his thoughts from wandering to the box in his jacket pocket. "What are you ordering for dinner?"

"Let's see." She looked to the menu and fingered each section. "For the first course, how about baked brie; second course, mixed greens; and the third, pan-seared chicken. And the side, mashed potatoes." She set the menu aside and caught him staring. "What?" She touched her cheek. "Kaylie mentioned my makeup—"

"You're beautiful, Julia. When I look at you, I'm lost. I'm

still amazed we're here after all this time. There's no other place I'd want to be but at your side."

"Does that include a garden in Fletcher County?"

The server returned with their drinks, stopping him from answering. He eyed Julia, trying to understand her question as she gave the server her order.

"Sir?" the server asked, watching him expectantly.

"Oh, yes." He quickly looked over the menu. "I'll have the charcuterie board, mixed greens, and tomahawk with mashed potatoes." The server collected the menus and left. "Julia, I hope you know that wherever you go, I'll go."

"Is that a yes?"

"Yes, without question. But why do I feel there's more to your question than what you're telling me."

She leaned into the table, her eyes brightening. "They called, Andrew. It was the reason I was late getting here."

His mind was spinning at what she was saying. "Who called?"

She chuckled, putting her hands on the table. "Fletcher's city council. They're interested in adding a garden in the area where I showed you. I have a meeting early next week to hammer out the details, but if it's approved, we could start clearing the land by spring."

Andrew covered her hands with his own and gave them a slight squeeze. "Juls, I'm so happy for you." The server headed their way with a tray, and he hated to be interrupted at this moment, so he paused in what he was saying. "The food's coming."

She sat back in her chair, meeting his eyes as the food was placed on the table. When the server walked away, Julia continued, spooning her brie. "You were right, the Lord worked everything out. Thank you for sharing about the garden. If it wasn't for you, I wouldn't have been able to change the city council's mind." She took a bite and smiled. "So good."

"There's plenty here on the charcuterie board for us both, so please help yourself." He cut up several slices of meat and cheese. "Julia, what you've been able to accomplish is impressive. The council needed to know, but I can't take all the credit. Michael also had a hand."

"It seems the Lord used Michael in the process as well as by telling you to find me."

"But don't tell him that," Andrew said around a bite. "He loves taking the credit. He's probably around here somewhere smiling to himself for how well tonight is going." Andrew instinctively thought about the box in his pocket, a surprise he planned after tonight was over and the cameras were shut down. Something Michael knew nothing about.

Julia tilted her head, questions flitting across her lovely features. "What are you thinking? There's a hint of a smile on your lips."

He mimicked the angle of her chin and wanted to run a finger along her freckle again and draw her close, though he held himself back. "There's something I want to ask you later tonight, but I want to wait until we've fulfilled our bargain with Michael."

"I'd like that," she said, her gaze looking out through the darkened windows. "I know I was young, just graduating high school, but when I lost you, it felt like my world had come to an end. Later, I realized it was because of the Lord's mercies that I wasn't consumed. His compassion and love for me didn't fail though at times I turned away from Him in hurt. Every morning, He was there picking me up and carrying me forward. He has given me the life He wants me to have."

"And I want to be a part of your future." He shook his

head to himself. This wasn't where he wanted to have this conversation. "I wish we could slip away to be alone."

She turned back to him and blinked, an unspoken agreement shining in her eyes. "Let's do it."

His pulse began to race. "Juls," he whispered and looked around. "The cameras will follow us. We're still technically on the clock."

"I don't care," she said boldly, clasping his hand. "I have a feeling about what you're going to ask, and I'm ready to start our lives together."

Andrew didn't need any more convincing. He stood from his chair and escorted her through the restaurant. At the corner of his eye, he saw and heard a commotion erupt as they entered the elevator and headed to the main floor of the hotel.

Julia held tight to Andrew's arm as they made their escape from the cameras to find a secluded bench outside. In the distance, a hotel light caressed them with a soft glow, allowing her to take a calming breath.

"Would you like to sit?" He ran his hand down her arm, entwining their fingers, before bringing her wrist to his lips.

How could she possibly sit? Her knees were about to give way at his gentleness, and if she moved a step, he'd have to lift her off the sidewalk.

"If you don't mind, I'd like to stand."

"Julia." Andrew reached into his jacket pocket, withdrew a black box, and opened it. "I love you. I don't know how long you want to wait to be married." He got down on one knee and lifted the box. "But I can't wait to be your husband. Will you marry me?"

She nodded, and unable to stay upright, she lowered to her knees in front of him.

"I need to hear the words, Juls," he whispered, tenderly kissing her.

"Yes," she breathed against him. "Even with the passing of time, my heart hasn't stopped beating for you." She chuckled softly. "This is the second time we've been engaged to be married."

He removed the ring from the box and slid the carat diamond on her ring finger, meeting her gaze. His eyes misted over. "It fits perfectly."

"Oh, Andrew, it's so beautiful." Tears threatened but she bit her lip to keep them at bay. She took in the row of small cut diamonds alongside the carat. "When did you have time to shop for this?"

"After I found you in the garden."

"A month ago?" She arched an eyebrow in surprise.

He gave a sheepish smile. "I wasn't sure if my prayers were finally being answered by seeing you again, but the moment you agreed to help me win my position as a morning show host, I knew the Lord's hand was in our meeting. After everything that happened between us, you were still willing to help me. From that moment on, I had the faith to move toward our future, in hope the Lord would make the way clear."

"Cut!" Michael broke through the hedges, startling them. "You were engaged before?! Why am I just now hearing about this." He stomped over to where Andrew was helping her stand.

"Michael." Andrew's voice was tight. He cut his boss a look, and she could tell he was keeping his tongue in check. "Were you listening?"

Michael shot him an answering glare. "It seems you keep your life close to your chest. You were engaged before? When?"

Andrew turned to her, his jaw tense as he ignored Michael. He placed an arm around her waist, holding her close. "Is our time up? Are we now free to live our lives in private?"

Michael ground his teeth and checked his watch. "Certainly."

"It's okay," she placed a palm on Andrew's chest, looking to him before meeting his boss's stern expression. "The City of Fletcher called this morning. They're interested in my proposal. I'm meeting with them next week. Andrew told me that you played a role in helping get more eyes on the project. Thank you. It means a great deal to me. And because of that, I'll share with you that Andrew and I were engaged once before." She went on to share her love for Andrew, what her dad had done, and how it had pushed the love of her life away. Then how years later Andrew had shown up to ask if she'd be willing to date him so he could win a job as a morning show host.

It was clear to Julia that Michael was touched by their past in the way he cleared his throat and looked away, but when he asked, "When do you plan to get married?" Her mouth fell open in surprise, but she closed it quickly.

"We've not had a chance to discuss it since we were inter-rupted, but once we do, you won't be—"

"I'm not sure." Julia cast a look to Andrew, and then to Michael, trying to calm the situation. "We've only been engaged for about ten minutes, but I'm thinking as soon as possible."

Andrew's jaw relaxed at her words, and his eyes softened. "You read my mind."

"Good!" Michael clapped his hands. "Let's get you

hitched. I have a minister, and with your sister here, there shouldn't be a problem. And in the great State of Alabama, you don't need a marriage license."

Andrew eyed Michael. "You have a minister here. Why?"

Michael smiled proudly, palming his heart. "I'm a man of romance, if you must know, the reason being a lawyer wouldn't work out, but I have great intuition. I had a feeling you planned to propose. You've been hush-hush lately about your time with Julia. I couldn't take any chances not getting it on film. If you wait to get married, no cameras. Get married now, well, you get the idea."

Julia turned to Andrew, and he was already looking at her with a single question in his eyes. "I've waited my entire life for you. I'll wait as long as you need."

She shrugged. "I've been in the camera's eye for the last month. I believe this is well worth the outcome, more than a morning show or a garden. Besides, we're almost forty. If we plan to try to have children . . ." Her words fell away, and embarrassment warmed her cheeks at sharing her deepest desire. She couldn't wait to have children with Andrew.

"Then marry me, Julia. Tonight."

"I'd love to." It was the craziest thing Julia had ever done in her life, but thirty minutes later at a park on the Tennessee River, with her sister by her side, she and Andrew said their vows.

"By the power given to me by the State of Alabama, I now pronounce you husband and wife," the minister said, smiling. "Andrew, you may kiss your bride."

"Happy to." Andrew wiped a fallen tear from Julia's cheek. He gazed into her eyes. "I kept my promise."

She closed the distance between them, his lips hovering above hers. "What promise?"

"The one from when we were in preschool. I told you that

you wouldn't get away, that I'd chase you for as long as it took."

"I'm so glad you did."

Andrew kissed her then, and the world fell away, but the knowledge of the Lord's faithfulness rose within her heart, followed by thanksgiving for all that He'd done to bring them together again.

Epilogue

Andrew entered into a commercial break, and, catching sight of Julia on the other side of the studio window, his heart quickened.

She came.

He hadn't asked her to, but he was learning more about his wife and how big her heart for others was, and especially for him. Her soft gaze caught his full attention. His lips parted in a smile, and she grinned in a "I'm proud of you" way.

The intercom crackled to life. "Drew, we're back. Dead air."

He hurried to flip the "On the Air" switch and chuckled into the mic. "Sorry about that, my wife is here, and while I've not been able to say hello, I was lost in her brown eyes." Within moments, every phone line lit with callers. He had had a constant stream of listeners congratulating him on his upcoming promotion to the morning show, but this had nothing to do with him.

He winked at Julia and accepted a call. "You are on the air."

"Drew, this is Mandy. Since today is your last day, can we get Julia on the air with you? I think your listeners, like myself, would love to hear you both together."

"Let me ask her." He pointed to her, to himself, and then to the mic. When she didn't respond, he continued with the show. "Mandy, I'm not sure . . ." Julia took a step toward him and nodded. "Oh, wait, she's coming. Hold on." He opened the studio door and pointed to an extra headset on the opposite side of the oblong desk. She put it on, and he showed her where to find the "on" switch.

"Hello, Mrs. Larsen. I'm so glad you're joining me," Drew said with a wide grin, enjoying the sound of her name on his lips. He was thankful his listeners couldn't see him because he was certain the emotions running through him were on his face.

"Hello, to you, Mr. Larsen. I'm glad to be here," she said, blowing him a quiet kiss. "How are you, Mandy?"

"Wow, Julia! I can't believe it's you! My entire family watched each show and couldn't wait for the next. I really connected with you and your willingness to help others. It's a great thing you're doing with your gardens."

Hesitantly, Julia angled closer to the mic. "Very kind of you to say, Mandy. If you're ever looking for a place to volunteer, check out All-Roads Garden's website. There's links to get you started."

"Thanks for calling, Mandy." Drew reached for the next caller. "You're on the air with Drew and Julia." He nodded. "I like the sound of that."

"Hey, Drew! Tay, here. I just wanna say thanks for the years. The 10–2 radio spot won't be the same without you. And Julia, you take care of our man, Drew. You got a good one."

Julia looked to him. "Don't I know it."

Drew laughed. "Actually, it's the other way around, but thanks for the call, Tay." His gaze roamed to the clock on the wall. "I wish we had time to say hello to everyone, but I see Rob is in the next studio ready to carry you through the drive home. Thank you for being a part of my life all these years. I enjoyed being a part of yours. Until next time, Drew and Julia, signing off." After shutting everything down, he caught Julia by the hand and pressed his lips against her knuckles. "My duchess."

"Are you a duke now?" She bit her lip to hide her smile, but the laughter dancing in her eyes gave her away.

"Now that we're married, I'm sure Stacey will promote us to our proper titles. Speaking of, we should go. If we're late, Kaylie will blame me." He held the door for her and led them out of the studio area and down the hall toward the elevators.

"I highly doubt that. You have my family wrapped around your finger."

"I don't see the problem." He winked.

"Drew. Julia." Michael peeked out from his office and headed for them. "Can I have a word?"

"Sure, we have a minute." Andrew placed a hand on her back, needing the touch. "What can we do for you?"

"I was listening to your final show and a thought came to me."

Andrew raised a brow, his suspicion growing. He could see the wheels turning a profit in Michael's eyes, and he wanted nothing to do with it.

Andrew slid his arm around his wife's waist and moved her toward the elevators. To Andrew's frustration, Michael followed.

"What do you both think about having your own show?"

"Michael," Julia said, shaking her head and moving them forward. When they reached the elevator doors, she pressed the button.

"We'll name it as you said earlier, Drew. The Drew and Julia Show."

"Sorry, Michael, but I won't have time since I'm hosting the morning show."

"It can be on another day. I'm thinking of a community radio program to amplify local voices, share inspiring stories, and promote local events. A full talk radio program. People already love you both. The calls were pouring in."

The elevator doors opened, and Andrew took a step, but Julia placed a hand on his arm, stopping him.

"A community radio program? Does the location matter? I mean, where you're broadcasting from?" Julia's gaze flicked to the closing elevator doors before settling back on Michael.

"Wherever you want," Michael assured, already anticipating her answer.

She looked to Andrew, then back to Michael. "Let's us think about it, then if it's something we'd like to pursue, we can talk terms. You'll have our answer within three weeks."

"I'm going to enjoy working with you both." Michael grinned and walked away.

Julia pressed the elevator button again before laughing. "Michael is something."

"To say the least." Andrew tucked a strand of hair behind her ear and ran a finger along her jaw. "Michael is full of ideas, but if this is something you'd like to do, I'll support you. I just don't want you to feel pressured into something." The elevator doors opened, and they entered and pressed the ground floor button.

"I'd like for us to pray about it, but this interests me. We could share heartwarming stories from the community, much like your first kiss stories. We can broadcast from different locations."

Andrew lifted her hand and pressed a kiss to her knuckles, then moved to her wrist. "You don't need to stop. I'm listening."

She moved her wrist slightly to the left, and he was happy to oblige. "I'm ready to leave tomorrow for our honeymoon. Are you ready?"

The elevator dinged, and Andrew straightened, clasping his wife's hand within his before walking through the lobby.

When he thought of his little boy heart from so long ago, there hadn't been hurt or pain there, only fascination with the pretty girl with pigtails. As time passed, he knew the emptiness and the hardships the world offered, but the Lord's hand was on him, guiding his path, leading him right to the love of his heart. "Absolutely."

Dear Reader

As an author, I enjoy creating fictional stories, but at times, I need to take a creative license and mix fiction with truth.

For truth, I used Birmingham, Alabama, for the home of Drew's radio station. But through creative license, there is the county and city of Fletcher, which are nearby in the story. The county doesn't exist, and to my knowledge, this city doesn't exist in the State of Alabama either. I created this location because when I thought of the place for the second garden, I pictured a mixture of places I've seen or stopped at while driving through the state. Yes, a small ice cream shop and a deserted detention area were very prominent in my mind, giving the story a wonderful visual description that didn't match a real place, so a fictional one was needed.

Another blend of truth and fiction is Drew's first kiss. The hide-n-seek game, the gate, a little girl getting hurt, the kiss—those are all true and from my past. It was actually my first kiss. I still have the scar from the fence after all these years.

The name of Julia's garden, All Road's Garden, points to my fictional historical romance series, All Roads Lead to Texas. Also, last year, for the nonprofit I work for, I started a community garden to help senior citizens fight food insecurities. And while our garden isn't as big as Julia's, it doesn't lessen the impact we have in the lives we serve.

I'll leave you with one final fun fact. The restaurant Michael reserved for Julia and Drew's date, 360 Grille, is indeed a real place in Florence, Alabama. While I've not been there personally, I've been talking to my husband about taking a trip. I'd love to go! If you've ever been, or plan to go, I'd love to hear about your experience. During the time of the writing of this book, it was one of the top ten restaurants in Alabama. The food looks divine and the scenery absolutely beautiful.

Thank you for reading Julia and Drew's story! I hope you enjoyed this bonus look at *Dial K for Kiss*.

In Him,

~Tanya

Series

Daisy Morton never expected her Grandma Ella's wildly popular buckeye cake business to fall into her lap. At twenty-two, Daisy faces a life-changing decision: move to Columbus as planned or stay in her hometown of Winterberry and put her skills to immediate use.

Jesse Graham only planned on sharing lunch in a little Ohio town with Daniel, his childhood friend. Instead, he's inexplicably talked into delivering decadent chocolate cakes for a girl named Daisy. Why does her name sound so familiar? Surely, he'd remember the most intriguing—and beautiful—woman he's ever met.

As Jesse puzzles over Daisy's identity, he accepts an offer to help Daniel's family remodel their home. With his parents long gone and his siblings living across the country, the lure of Winterberry's quaint holiday festivities and fun, quirky townspeople tempt him to stay.

When Jesse receives an irresistible job offer, Daisy knows God has bigger things in store for the handsome young entrepreneur. As much as she's come to care for him, Daisy must let him go. As for Jesse, if he leaves Winterberry, will he be making the biggest mistake of his life?

Check out the next book in the You Are on the Air series.

About the Author

Tanya Eavenson is an award-winning Christian romance novelist. She enjoys spending time with her husband and their three children. Her favorite pastimes are grabbing a cup of coffee, eating chocolate, and reading a good book. You can find her at her website, Facebook, or at her readers group, Tanya's Books & More.

Website
https://www.tanyaeavenson.com/

Facebook
https://www.facebook.com/TanyaEavensonAuthor

Also by Tanya Eavenson

Unending Love Series

Unconditional

Restored

Gaining Love Series

To Gain a Mommy

To Gain a Valentine

To Gain a Bodyguard

To Gain Forever

The Way We Are

All Roads Lead to Texas

The Rescue

The Proposal

Georgia Peaches Series

The Heart of Mercy

Whispers in Wyoming

Finding You